Skade and the Enchanted Snow

ALSO BY
JOAN HOLUB & SUZANNE WILLIAMS

Don't miss the latest books in the
Goddess Girls series!
Medea the Enchantress
Eos the Lighthearted
Clotho the Fate

Check out the most recent books in the
Heroes in Training series!
Dionysus and the Land of Beasts
Zeus and the Dreadful Dragon
Hercules and the Nine-Headed Hydra

Read more books in the Thunder Girls series!
Freya and the Magic Jewel
Sif and the Dwarfs' Treasures
Idun and the Apples of Youth

Be sure to read the Little Goddess Girls series!
Athena & the Magic Land
Persephone & the Giant Flowers
Aphrodite & the Gold Apple

Thunder Girls

BOOK 4

Skade and the Enchanted Snow

JOAN HOLUB &
SUZANNE WILLIAMS

Aladdin
New York London Toronto Sydney New Delhi

ALADDIN
An imprint of Simon & Schuster Children's Publishing Division
1230 Avenue of the Americas, New York, New York 10020
First Aladdin paperback edition March 2020

Also available in an Aladdin hardcover edition.

Designed by Laura Lyn DiSiena
The text of this book was set in Baskerville.
Manufactured in the United States of America 0721 OFF
2 4 6 8 10 9 7 5 3
Library of Congress Control Number 2019948051
ISBN 978-1-4814-9649-0 (hc)
ISBN 978-1-4814-9648-3 (pbk)
ISBN 978-1-4814-9650-6 (eBook)

For our fantastic readers.

Knowledge is power!

Annie W., Lori F., Irena and Emily and Maya, Ellis T., Layla S., Christine D-H., Olive Jean D., Eli Reuben D., Caitlin R. and Hannah R., Rose M., Kiaya M., Leila M., Kira L., Christina L., Aurora and Elia P., Malia C. and Olivia C., Natalie B., Allison B., Heather B., Denise D., Lorelai M., Aurora S. and Charlotte S., Andrade Family, Michelle H., Amari S., Latoya S., Reese O., Barbara E., Emily S., Steve S., Sara L., Kalista B., Claire B., and you.

—J. H. and S. W.

Contents

HLIDSKJALF
VALHALLATERIA
BREIDABLIK
VINGOLF HALL
ASGARD ACADEMY
ALFHEIM
ASGARD
VANAHEIM
WELL OF URD
DARKALFHEIM
MIDGARD
JOTUNHEIM
NIFLHEIM
HELHEIM
MUSPELHEIM
NIDHOGG
YGGDRASIL

Skade and the Enchanted Snow

1

Polar Bear Boogie

It was Thursday, and twelve-year-old Skade was in her fourth-period Norse History class at Asgard Academy. Concentrating hard, she spun herself in a tight circle, around and around on the wood plank classroom floor. Her long, thick, white-streaked black hair fanned out around her as she spun. Believe it or not, this was a history lesson. Dancing! And she and her classmates were all having a lot of fun with it.

Their teacher, Mr. Sturluson, had begun a Traditions

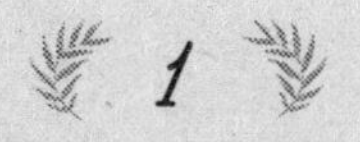

and Rituals unit this afternoon. They were learning the traditional folk dances of Norway, starting with one called the *halling*. They'd needed music, of course, so a boygod named Fossegrim was playing the fiddle. And another named Bragi was playing his lute, a stringed instrument with a deep, round back. To give themselves more floor space to move freely throughout the room, they'd pushed all their chairs and desks against the walls, which were slanted since the classroom was actually built to look like the inside of a big, wooden sailing ship.

Between each twirl she made, Skade folded both arms across her chest and squatted low on the balls of her feet. Then she'd pop back up to begin the sequence again. *Squat, stand, twirl. Squat, stand, twirl.* Occasionally, she and some of the girls in class would slightly lift the hems of their *hangerocks*—apronlike dresses they wore over linen shifts—to ensure they wouldn't trip over them.

Whenever the fiddle music hit a loud, hard note, students in line were supposed to take turns leaping

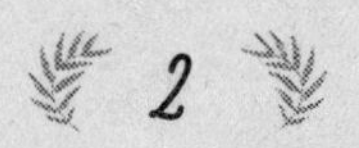

high to try to kick a black hat off the end of a pole. The other end of this pole was held by their bearded teacher Mr. Sturluson, who stood on a chair at the far side of the room. He held the pole horizontally about six feet above the floor so that its hat-covered end jutted into the middle of the room. So far, no one had managed to jump and kick high enough to knock that hat off.

Skade eyed it carefully as three boygods named Balder, Ull, and Njord, who were dancing in line ahead of her, waited for their turns to try. After them, she'd be next.

She breathed hard as she danced in place, squatting, standing, and twirling. As she pictured herself doing the precise moves needed to successfully dislodge the hat, her confidence rose. When it was her turn to be the one to try to kick that hat, she'd send it flying up to the rafters!

Although she was a good athlete, she'd never tried dancing before. There had been dances at her old

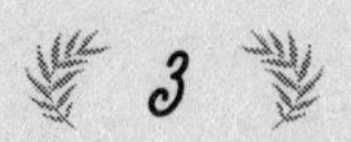

school to celebrate the changing seasons. However, she'd always skipped them in favor of going skiing—her favorite sport. Who knew dancing was such great exercise, though? And much to her surprise she had really gotten into the rhythm of the music. She'd definitely been missing out. Because she was loving the *halling*. And she was rocking it too!

As Skade executed another twirl, she recalled the posters she'd seen around the academy the last few days promoting a school dance this weekend here at Asgard Academy. Maybe she should go. Freya, Sif, and Idun would probably come with her. She and those three were all girlgoddesses with various magical powers. They'd quickly become good friends when the academy opened and they'd been thrown together as podmates (which meant they shared a room in the girls' dorm).

This was after Principal Odin had invited (ordered, actually) certain students from various places within the nine worlds of the Norse universe to leave their

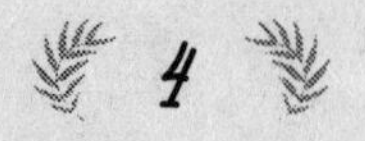

homes and schools and come enroll here at AA. And since no one ever said "no" to the supremely powerful Odin—not if they knew what was good for them—here they all were.

Skade stepped closer to the end of the pole that stuck out into the center of the room. The end with the hat. Only Njord, the boygod of the sea, remained in line ahead of her now. Fittingly, his shiny yellow hair hung in shoulder-length waves that kind of reminded her of seaweed. She watched as he spun, then kicked. And missed. He looked annoyed and embarrassed.

"Good try," she told him, attempting to lighten his mood as she continued breathlessly dancing. But instead of smiling at her, he straightened the leather cord necklace he wore that held nine small seashells, and sent her a sour look.

Boys! Why did they always seem to get majorly put out when they couldn't win every single contest, big or small? Still, she understood that in a way. Winning at

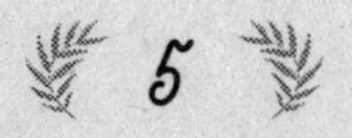

any kind of athletic competition was really important to her. Luckily, she often did win!

Finally, her turn had come to try to kick the hat off the pole. Eyes on her goal, she moved forward, her confidence running high. She could do this! She was going to nail that hat with one sharp kick-shot. *Squat, stand, twirl.* As soon as she heard the hard musical note, she reared back, readying to jump and kick her right foot high in the perfect strike.

Suddenly a concerned classmate's voice reached her ears through the music, piercing her concentration. "You think Skade's okay?"

"No, she's *not* okay. Obviously. She's dancing like some kind of crazed polar bear," another voice replied. She was pretty sure that second voice was Njord's.

Her focus broken, she faltered as she kicked toward the hat. And missed! "Ow!" she yelled as her foot connected with the pole instead.

The thrust of her energetic kick caused her to spin

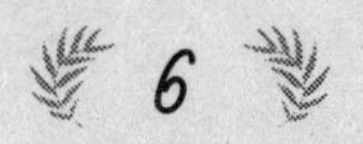

out of control and land in a heap on the floor. *Thunk!* Her hit to the pole dislodged the hat, all right, but only because she'd knocked the pole from Mr. Sturluson's hands. Before the pole fell to the floor with a *whap*, the hat rolled off its end to land at a funny angle atop her head.

Trying to make the best of an embarrassing situation, she grinned. Leaping up, she tipped the hat forward with one hand, swung her other arm wide in a grand fashion, and bowed. "Ta-da! I meant to do that," she announced.

At first there was only stunned silence. Then a few uncertain giggles erupted from her classmates. Her smile faded as disappointment filled her. All her confidence had been in vain. And she'd been dancing like a crazed polar bear? Is that what everyone thought? She flung the hat to the floor and glared at it.

After blowing her hair out of her face, she took a deep breath to calm down. "There's always next time,"

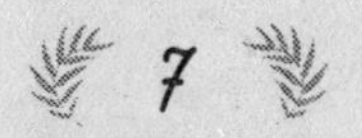

she muttered to herself. She was determined not to be a bad sport like Njord. Still, it wasn't fun to fail so spectacularly in front of the whole class.

Hearing murmurs, she glanced up. Numerous students had gathered around her. The looks on their faces ranged from confusion to surprise to amusement to worry. Probably because they were used to seeing her triumph at whatever athletic feat she attempted.

"Skade? Are you feeling *well*? Are you under a *spell*?" a boygod's voice enquired from behind her.

She knew without looking that it was Bragi. The boygod of poetry and music, he often spoke in rhymes without even trying.

"Um . . . er," she mumbled, unsure what to say. Usually she was outspoken and among the first to raise her hand or speak up in class during discussions. But feeling sheepish about her clumsy mistake (and maybe about her awful dancing style, if Njord was right about that), she found herself practically speechless for once.

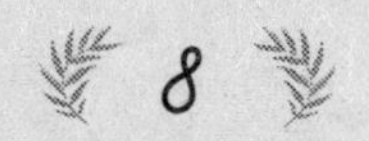

Mr. Sturluson, whose first name was Snorri because he tended to fall asleep easily and *snore* at his desk, had taken a moment to drag the fallen pole to one side of the room. Presumably so no students would accidentally trip over it. Now he came up to Skade. "You're never this quiet," he told her worriedly. "If there is indeed a magic spell at work here, we'll need a potion to cure you."

Although he looked and sounded alarmed, a yawn escaped him as he gestured toward a boygod with bright white spiky hair named Balder. "Go get the school nurse. Hurry!" he commanded. As though Mr. Sturluson's sleepy nature had affected him, Balder let out a yawn too. (Yawns were contagious, after all.) But then Balder's mouth snapped shut and he ran for the door to follow the teacher's instructions.

Seeing that the boygod was about to exit the room, Skade waved her arms. "Wait! I don't need a nurse. I'm not hurt and I'm not under any spell. I was just . . .

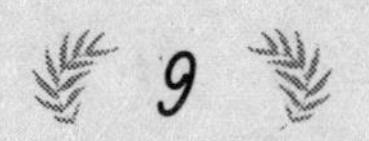

dancing. You know, like the rest of you guys." She took another deep breath, then admitted, "But I guess I'm not very good at it."

When someone snickered, she turned to locate the source. Njord again! Well, *that* stung. Instead of being part of the group, she was alone in the center of a ring of staring classmates. She hunched her shoulders. A few minutes ago, they'd all been having fun rocking out together as one big group. Now she felt like she didn't belong. That they were all looking at her as if they didn't really know her anymore.

Who is this bumbling, clumsy girl, and what has she done with the real *Skade?* she imagined them thinking. *Our Skade is a fantastic athlete and the best skier at the academy!*

Having retraced his steps from the door to stand beside Njord, Balder now piped up with, "I thought your interpretation of the *halling* dance was interesting, Skade."

Skade smiled at him and he smiled back. They

only had this one class together and hadn't ever really talked much, but she knew him to be nice and upbeat. His personality was so lighthearted that it caused his skin to give off a soft glow that matched his hair color.

A weird happy feeling moved through her as she studied him. *Huh.* What was that about? *Hmm.* Some of her podmates had crushes or almost-crushes. And she'd heard them and other girls talk about how they could make you feel melty inside. She hoped this wasn't a crush. If it was, she'd better crush it fast. From everything she'd ever heard, crushes were a big pain.

She knew this because her friend Freya was the girl-goddess of love and beauty. She received lots of letters from all over the nine worlds, each one asking for advice concerning crush troubles. *Troubles? Who needed* those*?* Not her! Anyway, these letters—which were necessarily short, since they were usually written with the pointed ends of fire-charred sticks on pieces of bark or large leaves—typically asked Freya things like how to get

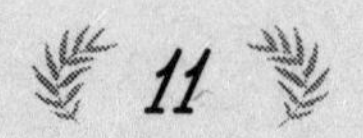

their crush to notice them. Or how to get over a crush who had hurt their feelings. *Why would anyone want to have to deal with that stuff?* thought Skade. Nope, she was *not* crushing.

She was brought back to the present when Njord snickered again. She watched him nudge Balder with an elbow. "*Interesting?* You meant her dancing was *hilarious*, right?"

Skade felt her cheeks turn red with embarrassment. While she'd been enjoying herself dancing, it seemed that others had been laughing at her—or at least Njord had.

"No, I meant interesting," insisted Balder.

Uh-oh, Balder being so nice was causing her to feel that happy-melty feeling again. Then she looked from Balder to Njord and it faded. She supposed Njord was cute and all, and maybe some other girl would get that kind of feeling about him. Not her, though. Not even for half a second.

"It's cool to learn dances from the olden days, but

what's wrong with changing them a little to suit our, um, *personalities*?" Balder went on.

He really was a nice boy, Skade thought warmly. Thing was, she hadn't been *trying* to change the dance, though. Were her dancing skills really so awful? Her athletic abilities had always been her biggest source of pride. She wasn't just the best skier at the academy. She was, in fact, the girlgoddess of skiing! Shouldn't she should be great at dancing, too?

"Unfortunately, that's not the lesson," Mr. Sturluson explained to Balder, drawing everyone's attention. "Class time is nearly over. Let's move our desks back into place for the next class. They've finished the dancing unit and won't need the floor space."

As the students began to do as he asked, the teacher looked over at Skade and frowned. "Skade?"

She blinked at him. "Yes?"

"Follow me, please. I'd like to speak to you for a moment."

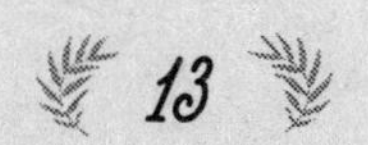

Was she in trouble? As the rest of the students began moving desks and gathering their stuff in preparation for leaving for their fifth (and last) period classes, Skade trudged over to the supply area behind a large shelf at the back of the classroom. She liked Mr. Sturluson. She didn't think she could bear it if she'd done something to make him mad at her. But if he was planning to scold her, at least he was doing it privately where other kids wouldn't hear.

"I won't keep you long," he told her, leading her to sit across from him at a table in the supply area. "I know you have another class to get to next period. However, I want you to think on something before you return here tomorrow."

When he interrupted himself to yawn big, she had to struggle not to yawn too. Yawns really were catching! "Our Traditions and Rituals unit is going to last for several weeks and will constitute one quarter of your semester grade," he went on. "So I strongly suggest you

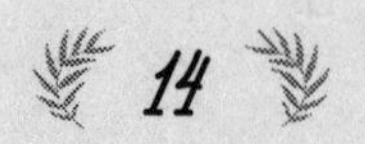

step up your efforts. You're usually a good student, but I don't appreciate you mocking the traditional dances in order to amuse your classmates today."

Her mouth dropped open in surprise. "Huh? But I wasn't m-mocking." How could he think that? Her stomach knotted in dismay.

Mr. Sturluson squinched his eyes at her. Then he folded his arms across his chest, looking like he didn't exactly believe her. "Really? It appeared to me that you weren't even trying to do the steps correctly. And what was that pratfall about? I fully expected you to be the one to knock the hat off."

Me too, Skade wanted to say. But the words stuck in her throat. A feeling of shame washed over her, even though she hadn't done anything wrong. Because she really *had* been trying to do the steps. Only apparently, she'd done them incorrectly. Her teacher would know that, of course. He was an expert on Norse History, and that included traditional dancing. He'd even written

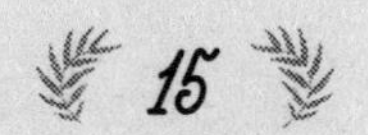

a famous scholarly book about Norse History called the *Prose Edda*. It was on the shelves of the Heartwood Library here at their school.

Skade was in awe of that book. She'd read it from cover to cover. It contained almost everything you needed to know about the nine Norse worlds. For instance, that they were protected under the branches of a single enormous ash tree named Yggdrasil. That tree was awesome. And magical! And it was the job of everyone it sheltered to keep it healthy.

"Well?" The elderly Mr. Sturluson cocked his head at her, causing his round red cap to dip and shadow his forehead. "Will you think about what I just said?"

Jolted back to the present, Skade nodded and then opened her mouth to explain that she really, really hadn't been trying to change the dance. But her words were interrupted by a loud *Toot!* sound.

"There's Heimdall's horn," noted the teacher, and they both rose from the table. Heimdall was the school's

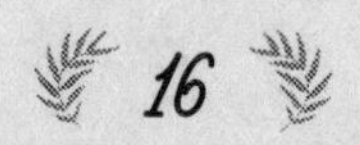

brawny, ten-foot-tall security guard stationed on a tricolor bridge called Bifrost that led to and from the world of Asgard. The bridge had been built from fire, air, and water—red for fire, blue for air, and green for water. And Heimdall guarded it day and night to keep intruders out of this world.

Mr. Sturluson's eyes had grown sleepy. He put his large hand over his mouth and yawned again. Afterward, he said, "You may go, Skade. I'll look forward to you working up to your usual standard of excellence in our next class."

Skade nodded. "Yes, sir." She had never been as happy to hear Heimdall belt out that end-of-class *toot* as she was right now.

Just as she was about to leave the small room, however, a series of additional horn blasts suddenly sounded in quick succession. *Toot! Toot! Tooooot!*

She and Mr. Sturluson both tensed in alarm. "The emergency signal!" they exclaimed at the same time.

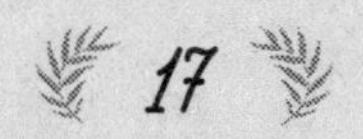

Along with the others who hadn't yet left, they ran for the room's ship-shaped exit door. Officially called halls, the academy's classrooms were basically individual tree houses set high among the branches of Yggdrasil. Instead of just the usual rectangles, their doors often took intriguing shapes and hung in thin air supported by magic, while the exteriors of the classrooms remained invisible to the eye until you actually entered.

Upon exiting now, Skade, her teacher, and her remaining classmates joined groups of students and teachers dashing from their classrooms. They all flooded onto the many small interconnected bridges that were offshoots of the main Bifrost Bridge. Which then led to a series of branch ladders, vine tunnels, vine swings, and vine slides. In combination, these allowed students to travel up, down, and around Yggdrasil to get wherever they needed to go.

On the branchway nearby, Skade saw students from

a class called Gnashing and Smashing launch themselves downward, many scrambling onto vine ladders that led to the path below. She grabbed a dangling vine, wrapped both hands and legs around it, and then promptly slid down to land safely on the fernway. From there she was swept into the rush of students weaving through a forest of golden-leafed aspen trees. They were all headed toward a great wall that, along with Heimdall's security on the Bifrost Bridge, protected Asgard from enemy attack.

Skade noted the looks of panic on everyone's faces. She could guess what they were thinking. The same worried thoughts she was. *Did Heimdall's horn signal the beginning of Ragnarok—a foreordained mythical battle they feared would one day end all nine worlds?*

At first, the aspen forest and Yggdrasil's branches grew too thick along the path for her to see whatever was happening ahead. But she could hear footsteps—loud ones—coming from outside the wall.

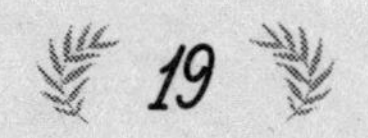

STOMP. STOMP. STOMP.

That sound could only mean one thing. Enemy giants!

"Here comes trouble!" someone yelled.

Skade feared they were right.

2

Frost Giants

THE STUDENTS AND TEACHERS OF THE academy scrambled up the steps built into the side of the huge, high stone wall that surrounded Asgard. This wall had been partly destroyed during a recent war but had since been fixed. From atop it they could all look down to the ground far below.

There upon the snow, three large figures stood next to a reindeer-drawn chariot. Skade recognized them at once. "Oh no!" she breathed.

"Frost giants!" shouted a black-haired, dark-blue-eyed boygod named Loki. Because he was standing right next to her, his voice hurt her ears. He'd almost sounded excited as he'd pointed out the trio. But then, this boygod trickster loved nothing better than trouble.

And knowing those three down below as well as she did, Skade figured it was *more* than likely they were here to make exactly that! Each stood about five times as tall as any of the girlgoddesses, boygods, dwarfs, light-elves, and humans who attended Asgard Academy.

"Giants can shrink themselves as small as any Asgard student when they want to," huffed a voice Skade recognized as Ull's. "They know there are rules against showing off bigness here at the academy. Which means they're just trying to scare us by appearing as humongous as they can!" Skade's eyes darted sideways to see that Ull, Balder, Njord, and Freya's twin brother, Frey, were standing just behind her left shoulder.

Other students along the wall murmured agreement

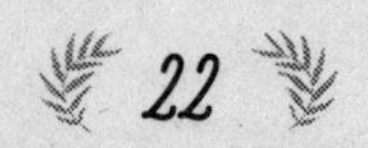

and began hurling insults at the giants below: "Show-offs!" "Bullies!" "Rule-breakers!"

Skade sucked in a breath. Hoping to calm the students around her, she called out, "Hold on! They may know Odin's rule that giants must shrink themselves when they visit AA. But they aren't actually on school grounds right now. So the rule doesn't count since they're *outside* the wall."

She knew a lot about giants and the way they thought. Because she *was* one! A half-giant, anyway, which meant she could only magically enlarge herself up to twice her current size. Her dad was a frost giant from Jotunheim. Her mom, a goddess of Asgard. Growing up, Skade had spent summers in Jotunheim and the rest of the year in Asgard attending a different school before being summoned to this academy along with twenty or more other half-giants and giants. Plus students from other worlds.

As the minutes ticked by, those three frost giants continued to stand alongside their chariot, arms crossed while silently staring up at the students and teachers on top of the wall. Skade looked left and right along the wall for her three podmates but didn't see them. *What are these giants up to?* she wondered. Could they simply be waiting for Odin and his wife—Ms. Frigg—to show up?

Just then something poked Skade's arm. It was Thor, nudging her with Mjollnir, his famous magical hammer. The red-haired boygod jerked his chin toward the giants. "Do you know who they are?"

She nodded. "The one on the left is Nott, the bringer of night," she said, pointing down at a beautiful grown-up giantess with midnight-black hair. Given what her job was, the color of Nott's hair had always seemed fitting to Skade.

Next she pointed to the giant on their right. "That's Dag, the bringer of day." He was a grown-up too and had bright sun-colored hair. Their chariot—the very one they were standing beside—flew them, the sun, the

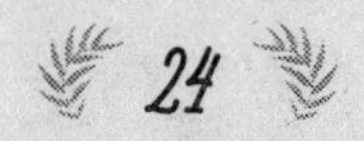

moon, and the stars across the sky, where they took turns creating light and darkness throughout the worlds.

"And that giant who looks about our age standing in the middle?" asked Ull.

"Skrymir," replied Skade, wrinkling her nose. He had nothing to do with day and night, so she figured the other two had simply given him a ride here for some unknown purpose. "Don't let his youth fool you," she went on. "He's highly skilled in magic and one of the sneakiest giants in all of Jotunheim. He can create illusions, making you see things that don't really exist.

"I remember this one time in Jotunheim, Skrymir made me believe I saw a pond coated with thick ice that was just perfect for skating. When I tried to skate across it, though, I discovered that the ice was actually as flimsy as cloth. *Crack!* I fell right through."

Somehow, gasping and choking, she'd managed to swim to shore. Skrymir had laughed like crazy as, shivering with cold, she'd climbed out. He'd never even apologized for his dangerous joke either.

"No way!" said Balder, looking upset on her behalf about that long-ago prank.

"Yes way," she said, nodding.

In truth, Skrymir kind of reminded her of Loki. She darted a quick look at that blue-eyed Asgard student and saw that he was studying the giants closely. Probably thinking up some sort of mischief. Since coming to the academy, Loki had caused plenty of that. He'd cut off her friend Sif's magical golden hair, for example. Which had resulted in the wheat crops in the human world of Midgard nearly dying off.

Another time, to save himself, he'd handed the super-sweet Idun over to an eagle-giant named Thiazi. Idun was the keeper of the golden apples of youth, which kept all the girlgoddesses and boygods at AA healthy and young. Though she'd eventually escaped, in her absence all of them had grown old practically overnight.

And that wasn't all. He'd once tried to steal Freya's magical falcon-feathered cloak!

Sure, he'd helped get metallic replacement hair for Sif, which had saved the wheat crops. And he'd brought Idun and her apples back in the nick of time to stop everyone from remaining old forever. Plus, he'd returned Freya's cloak. Still, Skade couldn't let go of the fact that he'd tried to hurt her podmates and then laughed it off. Unfortunately, despite his trickster ways, he was charming. As a result, he often got away with his pranks. Same with Skrymir. Which wasn't really fair.

"I've been expecting them, actually," Loki piped up suddenly, still eyeing the silent giants. Those nearby who'd overheard turned to look at him.

"Why? What do you know?" Thor demanded, and Skade saw him grip his hammer more tightly. It was so heavy that no one but this superstrong boygod could lift it. Anytime he threw it, it always did what he told it and then returned to him.

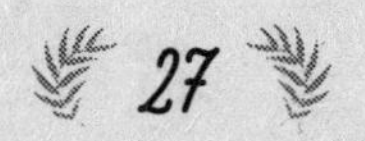

"Frost giants haven't been much of a threat since you acquired Mjollnir," said Loki. "But Odin suspects they've been regrouping. Maybe getting ready to wage an attack on one of the worlds." Loki thrust out his chin. "Since I've got a bit of frost giant blood myself, he sent me to do some spying, er, scouting. And I reported back what I saw to him," he added boastfully.

"Which was what? Tell us," Thor commanded.

Loki's eyes sparkled. "Sorry. Secret intel. Can't share."

At this, Thor snarled like an angry bear. Loki wasn't his favorite person. Not by a long shot.

Though it was true about Loki being related to the frost giants, he couldn't enlarge at all as far as Skade knew, even though he was a skilled shape-shifter. And he seemed to switch his loyalty between the worlds on a whim, depending on what fun there was to be had by choosing certain sides at any given moment.

Since Loki wasn't trustworthy in her opinion (or

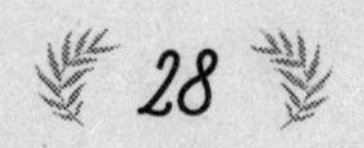

in just about *anyone's* opinion), she doubted his reports about anything. She was kind of surprised that a smart god like Odin would ask him to act as a scout. Of course, Odin knew better than anyone how sneaky Loki could be. So maybe that trait made him a good choice as a spy.

"Loki's told Odin whatever he found out. That's what's important," Skade reminded Thor, despite her doubts about Loki's trustworthiness. Her words seemed to calm the red-haired boygod, which was a very good thing. Because this boygod had a well-deserved reputation for having a quick temper!

"Are they ever going to speak?" asked Njord, gesturing to indicate the three still and silent giants below.

"I wish they'd just leave," said Balder. "If they're here to pick a fight, that is." Then to Skade's surprise, he yawned. Which seemed like a weird thing to do in the middle of so much excitement. It would only be normal if one were Mr. Sturluson.

"I'm just glad they're not fire giants from Muspelheim," murmured Frey.

Balder nodded. "Me too." Then he yawned again.

"Hey, are you turning into Mr. Sturluson Junior or something?" teased Njord, echoing Skade's earlier thought.

Balder looked sheepish "No. Sorry, I just haven't slept well the past few nights. Frey's right about the fire giants, though. Could be worse."

"Yeah," Skade agreed. So far the worlds of Niflheim, Helheim, and Muspelheim had all gone against Odin's wishes by not sending students to Asgard Academy. Skade and her friends couldn't help feeling rather glad about that. After all, Niflheim and Helheim were both realms of the dead. And Muspelheim was full of fire giants led by a cranky boygiant named Surt. She wasn't sure which was worse!

At this, Loki sent her a sideways glance. "I don't know. We've all heard that Surt's got a fiery sword that can do some pretty cool stuff. I'd like to see it in action sometime."

They all stared at him in shock. "Are you nuts?" Ull asked him.

"Yeah, that sword of his is supposed to be bad news," said Skade. Loki was the boygod of fire. Although unrelated to fire giants, everyone knew he had a strange, unsettling interest in them and their world.

Just then, there was movement on the wall as three new arrivals grandly made their way forward to confront the visiting frost giants at last. First came Asgard Academy's two principals, Odin and Ms. Frigg. Behind them loomed Heimdall.

Odin was easily recognizable by the black patch he wore over one eye and the two black ravens that perched on each of his shoulders. Aside from being principal, he was the leader of the Asgard gods and the supreme ruler of all the worlds, though not all the worlds obeyed him all the time.

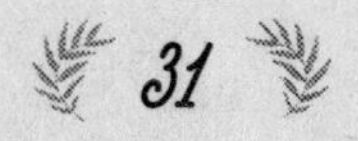

The tall, broad-shouldered, and brawny Heimdall gripped an enormous sword at his side, battle-ready at all times. His huge musical horn was slung across his shoulder by a leather strap. Shaped like a ram's horn, it was made of polished gold with etched markings decorating its length. Really, he was a terrific security guard. Just his frown was usually enough to scare off enemies. Not these giant visitors, though.

The crowd went completely quiet as Odin called out a greeting. "Giants of Jotunheim, why have you come to Asgard? What do you want?" At this the three giants frowned, looking even fiercer.

Ms. Frigg laid a hand on Odin's arm, and he stopped speaking. Her long blond braid shone brightly, as did her smile when she stepped forward to address the giants. "What Odin means to say is: Welcome. We hope you come in peace."

At her words, Nott and Dag turned their gazes to Skrymir. A crafty look came over his face. Although he smiled big, Skade wasn't fooled for one minute. She wouldn't trust Skrymir any more than she'd trust Loki! Did he think Ms. Frigg was a pushover because she was nice? Wrong. She was every bit as smart as Odin, which meant supersmart.

"Sure we do!" Skrymir's voice rang out. "Odin and Frigg, and all of Asgard, today I bring to you an offer of friendship."

Skade's eyebrows shot up. *Huh?* Since when did giants—particularly that boygiant—desire friendship with the gods?

"Skrymir is here representing the students of Jotunheim Academy in hosting a special sports competition in Jotunheim. It's this weekend on Enchanted Mountain," added Dag.

"Right. And I've come to invite some of *your* students to participate," said Skrymir.

"What kind of sports competition?" asked Ms. Frigg as Heimdall and Odin frowned suspiciously.

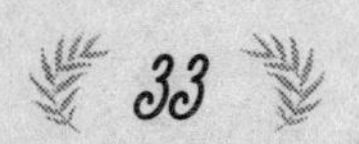

"If you'll allow us into your stronghold, Skrymir can discuss all the details," Nott suggested.

"We can listen to your offer from the top of this wall well enough," Odin informed him. "Please continue."

Smart move, Odin, thought Skade. It would be nice to be able to believe these giants came in peace, but she wasn't at all convinced. Unfortunately, most giants were still looking to settle old scores. Therefore, not all, but some, were a constant threat.

"Ymir's knuckles! What *is* this special competition? Just spit it out!" Thor shouted impatiently at the giants when no one responded to Odin right away.

At the mention of Ymir, the faces of all three frost giants turned winter-white and blustery. They leaned forward, fists tight. "Don't. You. Even. Mention. Ymir," growled Dag.

Ymir was a frost giant who'd lived in ancient times. After he died, the nine worlds had been built from him. *Literally.* Sky, clouds, mountains—everything had sprouted from Ymir. From his hair, from his fingers, from you name it. For instance, Midgard, the world of the humans, had been built from his eyebrows. Sort of icky, and Skade could understand why many frost giants were still kind of mad about all that.

As everyone knew, Principal Odin's purpose in bringing students from different worlds together at AA had been the hope that they'd become friends, thereby serving as a good example that might teach all the worlds to get along. Although life at AA wasn't all happy rainbows and unicorns, students were gaining a better understanding of one another. Still, right now she could sense old feelings of distrust between various Asgard students and these giant visitors swirling around in the frosty air and colliding like tiny pellets of hail.

"Explain your offer or leave!" roared Odin. At his booming voice, the ravens on each of his shoulders flapped away to circle overhead.

"Speak!" Heimdall growled at the giants. "The ruler of all the nine worlds is a very busy guy."

Ms. Frigg whispered something to Odin. Whatever it was seemed to calm him down.

"You'll have to forgive me," he said in a more moderate tone. "Recently I've gotten reports about suspicious activity in Jotunheim indicating that some there are gearing up to make trouble in Asgard. And now you arrive with this invitation." He quirked an eyebrow and gave the giants a piercing look with his one good eye. "So I have to ask myself, why the sudden interest in a special event to bring all the worlds together?"

"Because when Loki visited us recently, he reminded us that friendship among the worlds is what keeps Yggdrasil healthy," Skrymir explained. "And the good health of our sheltering tree means thriving worlds for us all." This information wasn't exactly news to anyone. Therefore, although he sounded earnest, Skade remained a little suspicious of his motives.

"So I came up with an idea," Skrymir went on grandly. "To host a one-day event I'm calling the First Annual Jotunheim Ski Games! We're traveling to every world inviting each to send a team of nine students."

Odin nodded, now seeming both intrigued and pleased. "Nine or a multiple of nine is always a lucky number." Stroking the tip of his long gray beard, he studied the three giants for several minutes.

The trio smiled big, waiting.

Finally, as if unable to bear Odin's scrutiny any longer, Skrymir blurted out, "There's no need to overthink this. Just say yes! It's a real opportunity. A friendly competition." Then he added slyly, "You're not chicken, are you? Afraid your students will lose against ours?"

Students and teachers on the wall held their breath and looked at Odin. Would he be angry at these rude and goading questions?

To everyone's surprise, Odin simply laughed as if

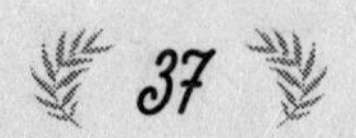

AA losing was a ridiculous idea to him. "We accept your invitation."

"Good," said Nott, nodding.

"Then we'll see you and your team in Jotunheim this weekend," called Skrymir. With that, the three frost giants leaped into the reindeer-drawn chariot and shot into the sky.

As they flew out of sight, Odin announced, "Students of Asgard Academy! Ms. Frigg and I will discuss this matter and get back to you soon with our decision regarding which students will represent AA at the ski games in Jotunheim this weekend."

With that, Odin, Ms. Frigg, and Heimdall departed, taking the stone steps down from the wall.

"We'd better get going," Njord said once they were gone. Skade and some of the others looked his way. "To class," he added.

"Oh yeah," Skade agreed. "With all the excitement, I forgot school wasn't over for the day. Hardly seems

worth going to our fifth period classes since there's only a half hour of them left."

Still, she, Frey, Loki, Thor, Njord, and Balder took off, scurrying up a branchway toward their fifth period class, Ragnarok Survival Skills. Along the way, all except Frey voiced the hope that they'd be selected for the Asgard ski team.

"I can't go," she heard Frey say. "After school, I'm going to tell Odin not to consider me. I'm heading out tomorrow with my Tree Lore class for a three-day campout to give aid to a field of blighted alpine bear-berries." The boygod of growing things, he took the welfare of the environment seriously, so it was no surprise he would choose this trip over the ski games.

Frey moved to walk alongside Njord, saying, "Do you have time to take *Skidbladnir* out to sea sometime in the next few days? It has to be sailed regularly or it starts making weird noises."

"Like?" prompted Loki, overhearing.

"Creaking and groaning mostly," Frey informed the group.

Hmm. Interesting. Skade hadn't known that about the magical ship. *Skidbladnir* had been given to Frey recently by some dwarfs. It was amazing, and anyone would jump at the chance to sail it. Choosing Njord for the job made sense, since he was boygod of the sea. So it was no surprise when he quickly agreed.

Frey pulled the folded ship from his pocket and handed it over to Njord to place in *his* pocket. The ship was only the size of Njord's palm now. However, when unfolded, it could grow big enough to hold a single person or an entire army.

Upon reaching their classroom, Thor pulled on the door. "Hey," he called out in surprise. "It's locked!"

"That's weird," said Loki. He rapped his knuckles on it.

While they waited for someone to answer his knock, Skade admired the dark, glossy door as she often did.

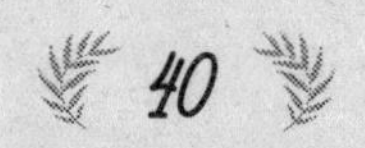

An image of Yggdrasil was carved upon it with its three fat rings spaced out one above the other to encircle its trunk like bracelets.

The first ring—the top one—included Asgard (world of the Aesir), Vanaheim (world of the Vanir), and Alfheim (world of the light-elves).

The second ring—the one in the middle—contained Midgard (world of the humans). To one side of that was Jotunheim (world of the frost giants), and to the other side was an underground labyrinth of tunnels and caves called Darkalfheim (world of the dwarfs). Skade smiled as she ran a finger over the carved mountains of Jotunheim. She'd skied almost all of them.

The third ring—the bottommost one—included Niflheim (world of ice and fog, where the dead went to be, well, dead); Helheim, a place run by the hideous female monster it was named for; and Muspelheim (world of fire giants), which was the most terrible world of all!

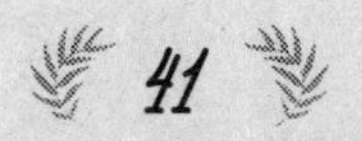

Could so many different worlds truly ever learn to all get along? Like Odin, Skade hoped so!

Since the door hadn't yet opened to admit them, she raised a hand intending to knock again when some students walking by on the fernway path below noticed them all waiting. "Didn't you hear?" they shouted up. "Odin called a meeting of all our teachers. They're over in Gladsheim Hall, discussing the Jotunheim Ski Games. So fifth period classes are canceled for today."

Instead of knocking, Skade grinned and punched her fist high. "Hooray! Time to hit the slopes!" she yelled.

3
Tryouts

CRUNCH. CRUNCH.

Minutes later, Skade was tromping up the slope of a nearby snow-covered hill, dragging her sled, with her skis strapped atop it, behind her. Her eyes twinkled, and she wore a big smile. Like most everyone she knew, she *loved* snow! And she especially loved snow *sports* like sledding and ice-skating. But skiing was her absolute favorite of all sports.

With each step, her red boots sank ankle-deep in the

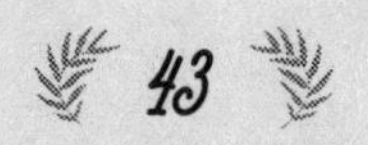

fluffy snow. Her breath made fog-puffs in the cold air of the late afternoon. More snowflakes drifted lazily down from the sky.

Others from her school were already sledding on the hill. Their joyous shouts rang out all around her. Everyone was having fun now, but things would get more serious at the upcoming skiing event in Jotunheim. She didn't think she was being stuck-up when she figured she was a shoo-in to make the Asgard team. It only made sense that the girlgoddess of skiing would be at the top of Odin's list, right?

As Skade neared the crest of the hill, her three podmates, Freya, Sif, and Idun, whooshed by on sleds, heading down. They waved, their hair streaming out behind them in the chilly wind.

They were laughing and hooting and calling out to her. "Woo-hoo!" "Look at us go!" "Come on, Skade. Join us!"

Skade had been planning to practice skiing first,

then maybe sled a bit. Instantly she changed her mind and decided to sled first, then ski later.

Grinning big, she punched a mittened fist in the air. “Yeah! Speed on! Make some noise, Thunder Girls!” Heimdall had given the four of them that nickname one day when they’d gone stomping across the Bifrost Bridge he guarded, and they’d loved it so much they’d hung a sign with that name outside their podroom in the girls’ dorm.

Huff. Puff. Skade began climbing the slope faster. She was in a hurry now to reach the top and sled down to join her friends at the bottom. Before the day was over, they would likely make many trips up and down this slope.

As she trudged upward, she passed some light-elves, with sparkly lights woven into their hair, who were building snow-elves. They were also having snowball fights and giggling like crazy. She smiled at their antics. They were always so happy. Watching them, you couldn’t help feeling cheerful too.

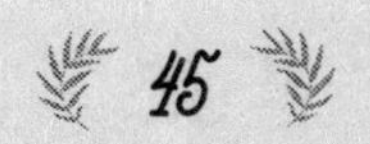

Laughter from students of all the various groups here at AA rang out across the hill, warming Skade's heart. Sports and games were so much fun that they made everyone forget their differences—at least for a while. Maybe it was wrong of her to be suspicious of those frost giant visitors' motives in putting together these ski games. Maybe their competition really would help foster friendship among the worlds. After all, this had been the whole idea behind Odin's desire to bring students from all three of Yggdrasil's rings here to attend the academy together. They were supposed to try to live in harmony, setting a good example for others outside of AA.

After finally reaching the top of the hill, Skade poked her skis to stand upright in the snow near some trees. Then she braided her hair to keep it from getting too tangled while sledding. Quickly she positioned herself on her sled at the hill's crest, her feet pointing downhill. A few yards away, she saw Loki talking to another girl, who was poised to take off on her sled too.

She was a frost giant with bright-white hair pulled into two corkscrew ponytails, one on either side of her head. Her name was Angerboda, which fit her personality just right, Skade figured.

Both of those two were troublemakers in their own distinctive ways. Loki played mean tricks, while Angerboda's anger often caused her to be just plain mean. Her fakey-nice attitude had a lot of students fooled, but when she was around Skade and her podmates, she dropped the act and was her true grouchy and spiteful self.

Regardless, it was only good sportsmanship to wish Loki and her well. So Skade nodded politely to the two of them. "Have a good run!" she told Angerboda. Then she leaned forward, using her weight to tip her sled over the crest of the hill. And she was off. *Woo-hoo!*

Out of the corner of her eye Skade saw Loki give Angerboda a push-off at almost the exact same time. Down the hill both girls zoomed. Cold air whipped Skade's long black-and-white braid behind her.

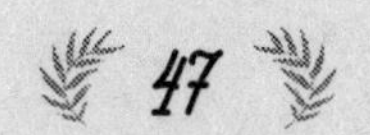

Glancing over her shoulder seconds later, she noticed that Angerboda's sled was angling in her direction at a dangerously high speed.

Oh no! Instead of pushing Angerboda's sled straight downhill, Loki must've pushed her *toward* Skade. And now their two sleds were about to collide! Hurriedly, Skade tried dragging her left heel in the snow to turn her sled away from Angerboda's approach. She was careful not to catch the toe of her boot in the frosty stuff lest she take a tumble. At the same time, she also leaned back hard to slow her sled. Maybe Angerboda's sled would be speedy enough to miss her and zip safely by.

It looked like her idea was going to work! That is, until a family of three moose ambled out of the woods on her left, directly into her path.

"Aghhh!" Skade veered away fast to avoid hitting them. Startled, the three moose leaped back through the forest of golden-leafed trees.

Phew! But although she'd successfully steered clear

of the moose, now she and Angerboda were again heading for a crash! She had three options. Crash into Angerboda, crash into the trees and rocks to her left, or bail from her sled before either of those could happen.

A glance over her shoulder showed that no one was behind them. So she wouldn't get run over if she bailed. Decision made, Skade leaned right. With a mighty heave, she launched herself from her sled! She hit the slope and tumbled head over heels. Snow went up her nose and into her mouth. Meanwhile, she heard Angerboda sail safely past. But just seconds later, she took a tumble too. They wound up rolling to stops only ten feet away from each other, their sleds perched at crazy angles on the rocks nearby.

Skade lay on her back in the snow, catching her breath. Her long braid was slung forward over one shoulder, and its tip lay across her upper lip like a bushy mustache. With a mittened hand she flicked it off.

"Skade? You okay?" she heard Freya call from

farther down the hill. However, she didn't reply or rise right away. She was too dizzy.

Another minute passed before Skade felt able to sit up. She gazed downhill and saw that her three podmate friends were now making their way toward her. Their gloved hands were cupped around their mouths as they called to her again. "Skade?" "Angerboda?" "You okay?" "Need help?"

"I'm fine," Skade called back, waving to indicate she was unhurt.

Angerboda sat up too, but she didn't answer Skade's friends. Frowning, she snarled at Skade. "Thanks a lot!" Then she turned her head and looked uphill, her expression embarrassed.

Skade followed her gaze. Suddenly there was a flash of bright yellow. Wearing his magic yellow shoes and skis, Loki whizzed by, spraying them with snow. "Oops!" he called back. His laughter echoed as he zoomed down the hill.

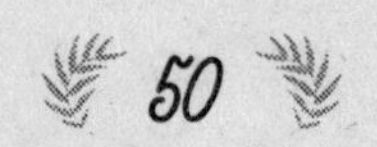

Skade glared at Loki, muttering, "What a weasel."

"He's not!" huffed Angerboda. Gazing after him, she sighed wistfully.

Ymir's eyeballs! For some reason, this girl liked Loki. As in *like*-liked. Freya was the one who had figured that out. She was good at guessing who was crushing on who.

Skade shook her head in disbelief. "Really? You're defending him after he made us crash?"

Angerboda pointed to their haphazardly parked sleds. "This accident was your fault," she asserted angrily, waving her arms in exasperation.

Skade leaned forward. "Me? What did I do?" she snapped. Since Skade was a half-giant of Jotunheim blood, Angerboda usually didn't take out her frustrations on her. But the more Skade made friends with non-giants, the snarkier Angerboda had begun acting toward her.

Angerboda sniffed. As if she had no good answer

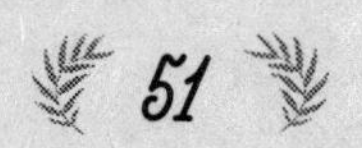

to that question, she gestured in the direction Loki had just gone instead. "Why is everyone always so down on him?"

"Uh, maybe because that boygod has caused no end of trouble since we got to AA? I'll just tick off a few examples, shall I?" Without waiting for a reply, Skade began to count on her fingers. "One. He cut off Sif's hair. Two. He stole Idun's apples. Three. He *tried* to steal Freya's magic cloak." She paused. "Should I go on?"

"Well, he managed to put all of those situations right in the end," argued Angerboda.

"Yeah, but only because he was pretty much forced to. He cannot be trusted. Obviously!" Skade jumped to her feet.

Angerboda did too.

They glared at each other, fists clenched.

"Wait up, Skade! We can do the next run down together," called a familiar voice just then. Idun.

Skade looked down the hill. Her friends were still heading up, getting closer now. Had Idun sensed that trouble was brewing between her and Angerboda?

Whatever. The interruption gave Skade and Angerboda time to cool down. "Okay! Waiting!" Skade called back with a wave.

Before Angerboda could start in again, a squirrelly voice spoke up from behind the two girls. "Big news!"

"Hó!" Skade exclaimed. It was an expression of surprise that basically meant, "Whoa!" She swung around to see a very large squirrel. He sat perched on a dark rock that was half-buried in the snow, twitching his tail in excitement.

She huffed out a relieved breath. "Ratatosk! Give a girl some warning next time, would you? Creeping up like that—you scared me."

The squirrel only grinned, displaying his two front teeth. Then he pulled something small, round, and brown from the knapsack slung over his back. A message acorn.

Ratatosk was always running up and down between the worlds delivering these acorns to spread gossip. Some of the gossip he whispered into his acorns came from an eagle-eyed eagle who collected news from its perch among the highest branches of Yggdrasil. But by the time Ratatosk reached Niflheim on the lowest ring of worlds and repeated the news to Nidhogg, the dragon who lived there, the squirrel had often scrambled things so much that the dragon thought the eagle was insulting him. So then the dragon would send back fake news, which would anger the eagle. It was this nosy squirrel's fault that those two were always arguing!

"Sorry. In a hurry. I've got *giant* news! News of *troublemaking* giants, that is." Giggling at his lame joke, Ratatosk tossed the acorn he'd been holding onto the snow between the two girls.

"Humph," said Skade. Unlike him, she didn't consider troublemaking giants to be at all funny. By the time she glanced up again, the squirrel was scampering across the snowy hill lickety-split while tossing message acorns to additional students.

"What do you want to tell us, you dumb acorn?" Angerboda asked meanwhile, stepping nearer to it.

"Shh! Be nice!" scolded Skade. Flipping her braid back over her shoulder, she bent forward at the waist to smile at the acorn in the snow, hoping to make up for Angerboda's bad manners. With their cute faces and hats and babyish voices, these acorns were a little nutty. But they were also fun and helpful. They delivered news (at least some of it accurate!) all over the nine worlds, wherever Ratatosk dropped them off.

"It's true. I do have *giant* news to tell!" shouted the acorn. It was circling the two girls now, rolling around one and then the other to trace a figure eight in the snow, over and over. Since sometimes they'd hop onto your hand, Skade offered her palm. But this one was too excited to stop rolling. It giggled. "Those giants that came? They brought an invitation," it informed both girls in its sweet voice.

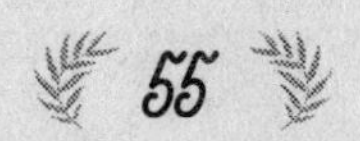

"Duh, we've already heard about their ski games," Angerboda informed the acorn.

Still, the acorn continued. "They'll be in Jotunheim!"

"Yes, we know," Skade said gently.

"But there's more!" the acorn sing-songed.

Both girls' interest sharpened. "What?" demanded Angerboda, stepping closer to it.

"Odin and Ms. Frigg. Watching everyone. Right now. Thinking. Deciding," said the acorn.

"Watching this very slope, you mean? To decide which Asgard students will compete?" asked Skade.

"Uh-huh," said the acorn in its babyish voice. As it rolled away, it called back a last bit of info. "Judging. On ability . . . attitude . . . academics!"

Skade's and Angerboda's eyes darted around their surroundings nervously. Skade had Odin's Eye third period. The focus of that class was on using a huge, super-magnifying telescope called the Eye that could flex and sneakily extend to gaze practically anywhere.

Which was how Odin was able to keep track of what was going on in all the worlds. It felt weird to know he might be watching—and maybe *judging* them right now.

"You and I are two of the best skiers at this academy," Angerboda muttered quietly, sounding worried Odin might overhear. "My grades are good, and I bet yours are too. But do you think us almost getting into a fight after our crash just now will disqualify us based on the 'attitude' category?"

She hunched her shoulders as if concerned Odin and Ms. Frigg were watching and judging them this very minute. Suddenly she smiled big and scooted over to hug Skade.

When Skade stared at her in shock and instinctively pulled back, Angerboda said in a worried whisper. "You'd better smile and look like you like me if you want any chance of being picked for the competition."

"Oh," said Skade, finally getting it and starting to worry too. Because . . . *attitude*. "Yeah, you're right. Just

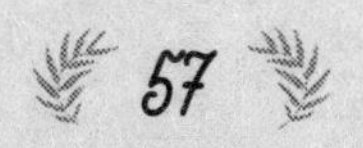

ing watched, we should at least pretend ong." Until the message acorn had spoken, she'd assumed that only skiing ability would determine who was chosen. But skill wasn't the only factor Odin and Ms. Frigg had decided to consider, it seemed.

"We're such good buddies, aren't we?" said Angerboda. Her smile got even bigger as she enveloped Skade in another hug. It was kind of scary.

Seconds later, Freya, Sif, and Idun came up to the two of them. Seeing the normally angry Angerboda smiling and hugging Skade, their jaws dropped in surprise. They were even more surprised when Angerboda opened her arms to wrap them all in a huge group hug.

"Great to see you guys!" she shrieked.

"Uh, yeah, hey, Angerboda," said Freya, looking bewildered.

Finally, Angerboda released them all. "Well, see you on the slopes!" she called in a too-happy voice. With a cute finger-wave, she left to retrieve her sled.

"Okay, that was weird," said Sif once Angerboda was out of earshot. "What's up with her?"

"She's trying to act friendlier to make sure she's chosen for the ski team Asgard sends to Jotunheim," Skade informed them before going over to grab her own sled. As they walked the rest of the way uphill, pulling their sleds behind them, she explained what the acorn had said.

"I think it's awesome that Angerboda's trying to be friendlier," Idun said as they tromped along. "Freya's brother's always saying how everyone should give *peas* a chance."

They all giggled at his substituting the word "peas" for the word "peace." Frey *was* always saying goofy stuff like that. Sometimes by accident and sometimes on purpose.

"Yeah," said Freya, flipping her glittery pale-blond hair back, "my brother says that *peas*, er, *peace*, is important for the survival of people as well as plants.

... the plants in our village in Vanaheim ...py during the war between us and Asgard."

"Trees are plants. So if Yggdrasil died, wouldn't all the worlds die too?" Sif asked worriedly.

As they finally reached the top of the hill, Freya slung an arm around Sif's neck and murmured, "Don't think about it. If those of us who live in the nine worlds can learn to live peacefully, Yggdrasil won't ever sicken."

Sif nodded, appearing somewhat calmed by her friend's upbeat words.

"Let's leave our sleds here and ski for a while," suggested Idun.

"Good idea. I mean, in case your acorn was right that Odin is watching," Freya remarked, looking to Skade right away. "Odin and Ms. Frigg surely know you're an amazing athlete and the best skier at AA. And the rest of us are pretty good too. But it wouldn't hurt to remind them."

Skade brightened at Freya's praise. An *amazing ath-*

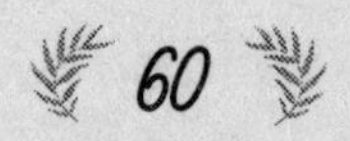

lete, though? It seemed obvious Freya (and probably Idun and Sif too), hadn't yet heard about her mess-up in Norse History class. She knew she shouldn't care if her friends found out she wasn't any good at dancing. Maybe being great at snow sports was enough. Right? She needed to stop worrying. And she knew just the thing to take her mind off of it. Skiing!

The girls leaned their sleds against some tree trunks, strapped on their skis, and took off zigzagging down the snow-covered hill among other sledding and skiing students. After warming up with a few runs, Skade left her friends and moved to the half-pipe area, which was dedicated to freestyle skiing. It was a U-shaped channel with vertical walls where she could practice fun aerial tricks and show off her skills.

She started with small jumps called pops and ollies. She did grabs in which she leaped, tucked her knees up, and gripped the sides of her skis with her hands. She did a shifty where she jumped, twisting her upper body

lower body the opposite way so her
at a diagonal. Then she practiced a harder
trick—a 180. To execute it she skied forward and then jumped and twisted in midair to land skiing backward on the snow.

As she skied to a stop afterward to catch her breath, she heard clapping and cheering. Looking around, she noticed for the first time that she'd drawn a crowd. Grinning, she did a goofy bow, which started others laughing and clapping even louder.

"Dinner starts in an hour. Let's head back, change into dry clothes, and put our ski stuff away," Freya called to her.

"Sounds good," Skade called back.

The girls quickly slipped off their skis, slung them across their sleds, and ambled off toward their dorm. Those around them had been visited by the acorn messengers too, and now she kept hearing the same words—ability, attitude, academics—drifting on the cold air.

Everyone was thinking about the upcoming decisions that would be made regarding team members.

Suddenly Skade's heart sank as a new thought came to her. No one could question her overall athletic *abilities* or her prowess as a skier. And she and Angerboda had probably rescued the *attitude* issue with their hugs.

But what about academics? Skade had always been an above-average student. Had today changed that, though? Mr. Sturluson had been pretty annoyed at her. What if her dance mess-up in Norse History caused her grade to take a hit? Could that disqualify her from competing in the ski competition?

4
The Team

ONCE INSIDE VINGOLF (THE GIRLS' DORM), Freya slipped off her red-and-white-plaid boots and set them on one of the racks in the mudroom. Sif and Idun did the same with their boots. Skade was so busy worrying, she forgot to remove hers. She started to push through the next set of doors.

"Stop! Boots off," her three podmates reminded her.

"Oops. I always forget," said Skade.

"Yeah, we know," Sif teased fondly.

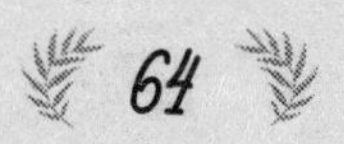

Skade sent her friends a sheepish look. They were always tripping over the boots and ski equipment she left lying around the room they shared.

After she took off her boots and stashed her skis and sled, the four of them padded into the main communal room in their woolen socks. A cheerful fire burned in a pit at the room's center, its smoke venting through a hole in the roof. They bypassed the game tables, reading nooks, and gathering spaces positioned around the roaring fire and made a beeline for their room. It was one of eighteen sleeping pods of various sizes, which were spaced all along the edge of the circular main room, like petals growing outward from the center of a flower.

The four girls heard giggles as they traipsed by a pod. There were six light-elves inside, all twirling in circles and having so much fun they didn't notice them pass. Each pod contained hammocklike podbeds and closets for four to eight girls, one small window, and a large floor rug woven with the big initials AA, for Asgard Academy.

"You look worried," Idun noted, searching Skade's expression as they trooped into their pod. The fire was making the dorm rather warm, so Sif went to open the shutters over their window to let in some air.

Skade flicked a glance at Idun, shrugging. "I just wish I knew for sure if I'm going to get into the competition. I mean, I know I'll qualify on athletics. I'm the girlgoddess of skiing after all. But that's only one third of what I need. And sports are so important to me, you know? I really, *really* want to be on the team."

"Hey, I've got an idea!" said Freya. Standing in the center of their podroom, she lifted her hand toward the nine necklaces that hung in a big, swoopy smile shape across her chest from one shoulder strap of her dress to the other. Each held a drawstring pouch that contained a curious object of some sort. Inside one, there was a cat's-eye marble that could magically transform into a flying cart pulled by two gray tabby cats!

Only one of the necklaces *didn't* hold a pouch, and it was Freya's favorite. Made of hammered gold, it had fancy designs and was decorated with small, winking rubies and diamonds. From its center dangled a teardrop-shaped, walnut-size jewel named Brising.

"Even though I'm sure the answer will be yes," Freya said to Skade, "I'll ask Brising if you're going to be chosen for the competition. Then you can stop worrying."

Brising was a magical jewel with the power to speak fortunes. Grasping it, she now asked: "Brising, will Skade be chosen for the ski team?"

Freya cocked her head to listen for the jewel's reply, then frowned, looking a little confused. Since only she could hear Brising's rhyming predictions, she repeated its words aloud for her podmates a moment later. "Brising says:

'Skade has an excellent chance,

if only she could learn to dance.'"

Idun looked up from removing her wet wool mittens. "Dance?" she echoed.

"Yeah, I don't get it. How would dancing help her?" Sif asked as she opened her closet to change from her damp *hangerock* into a dry one.

"I'll ask," Freya said. Then she repeated Sif's question to her magic jewel.

Skade stayed mum, waiting to see what the jewel would say, but apparently Brising had nothing more to share. Freya let the now-silent jewel fall back to rest on the front of her *hangerock* and looked curiously over at Skade as she went to her small closet to change clothes.

Should I tell my friends about today's dancing disaster? Skade wondered.

Before she could decide, Freya spoke up again. "Wait! Does this have anything to do with the Norse History *dancing* Mr. Sturluson has had us all doing in his classes?"

Sif's eyes lit up almost as bright as her golden hair. "Ooh! That's been sooo fun. But, yeah, what is Brising talking about? What's dancing got to do with being chosen for the competition?"

After pulling off her sweater and poking her head through the neck of fresh one, Skade shot her friends a nervous glance. But still she said nothing.

Freya blinked at her. "Well?"

"Um, what Brising said probably has something to do with my history grade, actually," Skade admitted at last. "Mr. Sturluson didn't like my dancing today. Not at all. Thought I was making fun of traditional Norse dancing. And the Traditions and Rituals unit is a quarter of our semester grade."

"You can't dance?" Sif asked, looking stunned by this information.

Skade sighed. "Apparently not." With that, she sat on her hammock and flopped onto her back with an air of doom. Either end of the six-foot-long podbed was attached by ropes to sturdy hooks in the ceiling, and her weight sent it swaying. The dorm's *pod*beds were in fact giant seedpods, minus the seeds. Where once a seed had nestled, now a girl slept. As did the boys over in their dorm, Breidablik.

After hanging up her mittens to dry, Idun grinned at Skade. "You've got to be kidding." Going over to her, Idun gently bumped her hammock with her knee.

Skade sighed. "Wish I was."

Idun's eyes widened. "But . . . but you're an athlete. And dancing's easy."

"Maybe for you guys," Skade said dejectedly.

"But you should be a natural at dance," Sif added, coming over too. "You've always been able to make any sport look easy."

Considering this, Skade let out another big sigh. "Maybe that's my problem. Maybe I think of dancing like a sport I'm trying to win?"

"Hmm. Makes sense," said Freya. "Why don't you

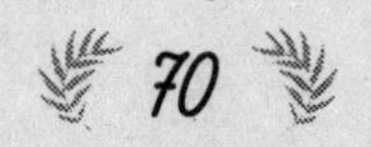

try to go with the flow instead? Relax. Feel the beat of the music. C'mon, we'll show you."

"All right." Leaping up enthusiastically, Skade scurried for the door. "I'll go get my boots."

"Wait! It'll probably be easier to learn in just your socks," said Freya.

"Boots are pretty clunky for dancing lessons," Idun explained.

Sif nodded in agreement, causing her long, golden metallic hair to swing at her shoulders.

Turning back, Skade studied her roomies as they began singing a well-known Norse song and dancing around the room to its beat. Leaping, clapping, and shimmying, they made the steps look so easy. And fun! After watching a few minutes, Skade joined in, trying to mimic parts of what they were doing. At times, three of them would boogie in a circle and one would jump into the middle of it to twirl and whirl like a star. They'd take turns showing off a move, then the others would try copying it.

"You're getting better already, Skade!" Freya declared breathlessly when they were done.

"Yeah!" Sif and Idun agreed.

"Yeah?" Skade echoed. She looked at her friends' faces, all rosy from exertion, and saw they were telling the truth. Maybe she wasn't doomed after all. "You know, I think this dancing stuff might help me with balance and style, which would come in handy for skiing. Plus, it's kinda fun."

"So maybe you'll even go to the school dance this Saturday night with us?" Sif suggested.

"I was just thinking I might!" said Skade, already feeling more confident. However her friends' insistence that she was dancing "better" didn't mean she now excelled at it. So, before they could get too excited, she added, "We'll see, though."

All the exercise they'd had that day had worked up the girls' appetites. So although it was a little early for dinner, they headed for the school cafeteria, known as the Valhallateria.

As they walked along the fernway, Skade had new pep in her step. The competition wasn't till Saturday. Tomorrow was Friday, so hopefully during class she'd be able to show Mr. Sturluson how hard she was working to master some dance moves. Realizing how much she was trying, he'd just *have* to give her a passing grade. Which would surely fix any academic concerns Odin and Ms. Frigg might have. And seal the deal on sending her to Jotunheim to compete on the AA team!

When the girls came to a place where the path narrowed, Skade dropped back a few steps to walk behind her friends. She practiced some of the moves they'd shown her, dance-walking and humming a little song. Suddenly she heard voices at some distance behind her. A group of boys were coming up the same path to the Valhallateria, and they'd been watching her practice!

Njord laughed. "I told you. She's terrible, right?"

"Yeah, I see what you mean," snickered Loki. "Totally like a crazed polar bear."

Out of the corner of her eye, she saw those two boys mock her movements. Confident Skade would have confronted them about their mean behavior. But not-so-confident-now Skade just walked on, feeling like she'd been punched in the gut.

"Knock it off, guys. She's not that bad. And I think she might've heard you," said a third voice. *Balder's.*

Skade's feelings were so hurt she didn't know what to do. She couldn't let them know she'd heard. It would be too embarrassing. After a few seconds anger began to simmer inside her, mixing with the hurt. How dare they make fun of her! Unsure how to handle these confusing feelings, she stuffed them deep down inside to think about later when she was alone. Catching up to her three podmates, she joined in their chatting the rest of the way to the Valhallateria.

Once inside, they walked past tables and chairs that had legs made out of bent metal spears. The chairs' backs and seats were formed from two thick wooden

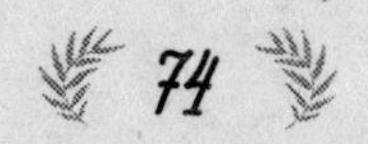

shields set at right angles. And the superhigh ceiling was tiled with hundreds more shields and spears made of shiny, dazzling gold.

Fantastic wooden friezes, which were basically huge sculpted paintings done in bright colors, covered the cafeteria's walls. The carved scenes showed hundreds of heroic-looking warriors feasting and marching. The Valhallateria was truly awesome! Just the sight of it and the smell of food lifted Skade's mood.

Right away, she and her friends headed for the goat-shaped ceramic fountain standing on a table in the middle of the room. It stood upon a pedestal shaped like a stout tree trunk. Green-painted leaves formed a flat, rectangular tabletop below it. Although it was early, many students were already here. No doubt everyone was extra hungry from their exercise on the slopes today.

Usually, cool, tart, sparkly apple juice poured out of spigots on all sides of the goat into a trough. But now the juice spilling from it was so hot, it was steaming.

Skade stared at it in surprise, then looked over at Idun questioningly. This juice was made daily from her golden apples of youth. She tended the grove where they grew and was the only one who could pick the apples. If anyone else tried, the apples would wither and die!

Idun grinned, "getting" Skade's silent question. "Since it's extra cold today and most everyone has been outside in the snow, I thought hot apple cider would be appreciated."

"You're so right," said Sif. The girls all grabbed *hrimkalders*—short cups with rounded bottoms—and filled them.

Skade blew on her cider to cool it a bit, then took a sip. "Mmm, that's yummy," she said, closing her eyes and smiling. A warm feeling filled her, soothing the hurt from Njord's and Loki's earlier comments.

When she opened her eyes again, her gaze fell on a small glass dome affixed to a tall, square wooden

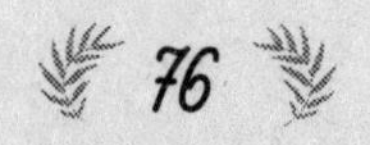

column beyond the goat fountain. There was a large button under it labeled with the words:

X540
Push only
in the event
of Ragnarok

X540 referred to an alarm—540 blasts—that would sound loudly enough to warn all nine worlds if the doomsday known as Ragnarok ever came about. Skade shuddered just thinking about that scary possibility.

"What's up with you and Njord?" asked Freya, nodding toward where he sat at a table with Loki, Balder, and some other boygods. "He's staring at you."

Before she could think better of it, Skade glanced over at Njord. For a fraction of a second, their gazes met. She bugged her eyes out at him, then looked away.

"Nothing. I don't know what his problem is. He's just started . . . *annoying* me all the time," she told Freya. Thinking of how he'd teased her about her dancing in class and also on the fernway a few minutes ago made that punch-to-the-stomach feeling flare up again. Quickly she took another sip of her cider.

"C'mon, let's go sit," said Sif, gesturing at a nearby table.

"I think I'm going to file Njord in the weasel category along with Loki. In my head, I mean," Skade said to her friends as they walked over to claim a table. Abruptly recalling that Njord and Freya had both come to AA from the same village in Vanaheim, she glanced over at Freya, hoping that Njord wasn't a close friend of hers.

"Why?" Idun asked in surprise. "What did he do exactly?"

Shrugging, Skade set her drink on the table and pulled out a chair as her friends were doing. "He just . . . you know . . . *teased* me."

Freya's blue eyes lit up. "Hmm. Boys often tease the girls they like. You do know that, right?"

"He does *not* like me. I'm positive of that." Skade

stared at Freya, not wanting to explain that Njord's teasing had not been the cute friendly kind, but rather the mean kind. At least, it had felt that way to her. Still, her friends didn't look convinced.

"Well, maybe he's jealous of your skill at sports?" suggested Sif. "He's pretty competitive, I think."

Skade let out a long sigh, not really wanting to admit that he had mocked her dancing.

To her relief, her friends got distracted when a boy-god named Honir called to her just then from two tables away. "Hey, Skade, think you're going to make the team?" She looked over to see a group of boys seated with him that included Frey and Ull.

"Does a bear poop in the woods?" Skade replied, grinning at Honir. Then she crossed her fingers behind her back since she wasn't really as confident as she'd pretended to be.

Honir looked confused. "What does bear poop have to do with getting on the ski team? Yuck. I hope I don't step in any on the way to Jotunheim. 'Cause I bet you and me and Ull will all make the team." Honir was a little (okay, a lot) clueless sometimes. However, he was one of the top skiers at the academy, so he was likely right to assume he'd be chosen to compete.

"Ew!" said Freya, scrunching her nose at Honir, and then at Skade. "New rule. No poop talk in the cafeteria. Or anywhere else." Which made Skade, Idun, and Sif laugh.

"Honir's right, though," Sif told Skade. "You two and Ull are probably AA's top skiers, so the three of you are bound to make the team. I mean, even if you aren't a dancing star yet, I think Odin and Ms. Frigg will give you a pass. Especially after you show Mr. Sturluson tomorrow in class that you're getting better and trying."

"Hey! Want me to help you put together the perfect outfit for the competition?" Freya asked Skade eagerly. Her eyes went slightly out of focus, and a dreamy look filled them as her imagination stirred. "I can see it now. I

could lend you my brown-and-gold tunic. The one with faux fur sewn on the shoulders. It'll go great with your olive green leggings."

Idun giggled. "Trust the girlgoddess of love and *beauty* to be thinking fashion forward thoughts about a sports event. That outfit does sound cute, though."

It was true. Not only could Freya put together amazing looks with the contents of her closet, but she could also design and *sew* clothes and accessories. She had more outfits than anyone else they knew!

"That sounds perfect," Skade told her. "Thanks. Ooh! I'm getting more and more excited about the competition." Of course she'd be chosen, she told herself, like everyone figured. But who would the other eight be?

Just then, Odin and Ms. Frigg entered the Valhallateria. A surprised hush fell over the room since they rarely came here.

"Students of Asgard Academy! May we have your

attention for an announcement?" Odin called out grandly. "We have chosen the nine who will go to the Jotunheim Ski Games."

Skade's eyes widened as gasps and murmurs filled the room. "What?" she whispered. "But . . . but . . ." Like the others, she'd assumed this announcement wouldn't be made until tomorrow after classes.

From all around her came the sound of chairs scraping the floor. Everyone hopped up in excitement and moved to surround the coprincipals so they'd be able to hear better. She crossed her fingers, hope, hope, hoping.

"Our team will include nine competitors plus a tenth alternate, in case someone is injured," said Odin. "Team members have been carefully selected based on ability, attitude, and academics."

"Since you've all been attending the academy for some weeks now, we are familiar with your athletic abilities," Ms. Frigg continued. "Many of you are talented athletes, and we had a large list to choose from."

"However, this competition isn't just about skiing skill," said Odin. "It's also about fostering friendship among the worlds. The team we send must be able to make friends and not cause trouble."

"That lets Loki out," someone in the crowd muttered, too quietly for the coprincipals to hear. In Skade's opinion, they were right about Loki!

"Feelings will be running high in Jotunheim. No world wants to lose, but some will and all must remain gracious in defeat," Ms. Frigg went on.

In competitions many individuals and/or teams sought to win, Skade knew. On the one hand, that kept everyone's skills in tip-top shape. On the other hand, it could create jealousy and hard feelings among those who lost.

Angerboda had moved to Skade's side while Odin and Ms. Frigg were speaking. Now she leaned over to murmur something. "Speaking of losing, you'd

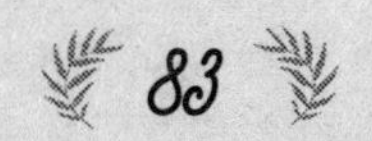

better hope that Helrun isn't part of the competition in Jotunheim. It really defeated you a few years ago, remember?" Since Angerboda was already cautioning her, the girlgiant obviously assumed Skade would make the team. Which was kind of nice. Except her words did cause Skade some concern.

Helrun was a ski run named after the world of Helheim. The run was sometimes misty, sometimes sunny, and always slick with ice. It was steep, narrow, and straight. And therefore terrifying, just like Helheim. Skade had been really tired the day she attempted to ski it a while back, and she had taken her worst spill ever on that difficult run. She'd wound up sliding backward and tumbling the last half of the way down it, head over heels. She'd never tried it again.

Trust Angerboda to cast a dark cloud over things. She knew this girl was just trying to undermine her confidence. (And it was kind of working.) But worse was yet to come.

"And lastly, after judging for ability and attitude, we looked at contenders' academics," Odin was saying. "We consulted with teachers to be sure those who are chosen are maintaining high grades in all classes."

At this, Skade gulped, wondering what Mr. Sturluson had told Odin and Ms. Frigg about her.

Odin cleared his throat importantly. His good eye swept the room. Skade squirmed when it seemed to land on her for just a fraction of a second. Then he looked down at a list in his hand. "The nine competitors representing Asgard Academy will be as follows," he announced. "Balder, Freya, Honir, Thor, Njord, Yanis, Malfrid, and Angerboda. Plus Ull, who will be captain." He paused and looked up from his list. "Our alternate will be Skade."

5
Nightmares

SKADE STOOD IN THE VALHALLATERIA frozen in horror. *Alternate?* She—the girlgoddess of skiing—was going to Jotunheim, but wasn't going to get to compete as part of the team? This. Could. Not. Be. *Happening!*

And yet it had happened. The team had been selected sooner than she'd expected. She hadn't had time to change Mr. Sturluson's mind. And now it was too late. A done deal.

All around her, cheers and squeals of excitement rose from those who'd been chosen for the ski team and those lucky students' friends. At the same time it felt like every pair of eyes in the Valhallateria was on her, as everyone (herself included!) wondered exactly why she'd been overlooked for the main team.

Only a part of her listened to the rest of Odin's remarks as he spoke about how AA's team would depart tomorrow, Friday morning, for Jotunheim so as to arrive in time for practice runs with all the other worlds' teams. And how the competition would officially begin Saturday morning and end by dusk. Another part of her mind was whirling with disbelief and humiliation.

Skade's three podmates gathered around her. They hugged her and murmured words of comfort and support.

"I can't believe this," Freya said, looking stunned. "How could I make the main team when you didn't, Skade? It's crazy!"

Skade tried to be a good sport. And she was truly happy for Freya, though she would've liked to be on the team *with* her, of course. "I can totally understand you getting chosen. You get along with everybody," Skade said. "And part of these ski games is about fostering world friendship. Plus, you're a great skier, quick and light on your feet, er, skis."

"But I'm not the *best*. And, I mean, Ull is the boygod of snow, so I guess he makes sense as a captain choice. Still, you're the *girlgoddess of skiing*! You should have been made captain instead," said Freya.

"Freya's right," Sif agreed. Then she nodded toward a group that included three of the boys on Odin's list. "Most of the other skier choices make sense, though. Honir's long legs make him superfast, Njord is nimble, and Thor's strength gives him great endurance." Thor happened to look her way just then, and she sent him a cute little wave, no doubt glad he'd been chosen. They were very good friends and almost-crushes.

"Yeah, and Yanis and Malfrid are supersweet, and quick, too. And everybody adores Balder, so they'll all be good representatives from our world," said Idun. "Plus Balder's skin has that cool faint glow. Could be a big help to our team on any slopes that are heavily treed and therefore dark."

"But Angerboda?" said Freya, holding her palms upward to indicate confusion. "Why choose her?"

"Good question," said Sif. "Sure, she's a great skier. But she's a troublemaker. Odin must know that."

Idun nodded, as they all glanced across the room at that girlgiant. Angerboda wore a fake-looking smile and was just then sidling up to Odin and Ms. Frigg. Probably to thank them for choosing her.

"Hmm. That girl's been acting extra nice to teachers lately," noted Sif. "It's kind of suspicious, if you ask me."

"Yeah, it is," mused Skade. "It's almost like she knew about this competition before anyone else did. I haven't

been to Jotunheim for a while, but she went for a visit a week ago."

Idun's brows flew upward. "You think she somehow heard in advance about the competition from someone there?"

"It would explain why she's been acting so goody-goody recently," said Freya.

A flash of anger at Odin overwhelmed Skade for a moment. How could he have fallen for Angerboda's fakey niceness? She wasn't nice! And he should have figured that out. After all, he was the smartest guy in all the worlds, except maybe for their school librarian, Mimir. So how could Odin have let himself be tricked into choosing Angerboda for a spot on the team? Skade just didn't get it.

With her confidence at an all-time low and feeling embarrassed and sad, Skade still knew how to summon up her inner team spirit. So she forced herself to do what she knew was right.

"Excuse me a sec," she said to her friends. Although she really, really didn't feel like it, she made herself go over and congratulate each of the other students who'd been selected as team members, besides Freya and her. "I'm so excited and happy to be part of this team. We're going to do great," she told them.

Angerboda left Odin and Ms. Frigg and wandered over to the group. After Skade quietly (and with great difficulty) congratulated her, too, Angerboda responded by giving her a big, gloating smile. "Gosh, thanks! And congrats to you for being named *alternate*."

Mortified by the snarky girlgiant's deliberate emphasis on "alternate," it took all of Skade's inner strength to simply murmur, "Thanks," and to walk away.

As she did so, she noticed Loki lurking close by. At the moment he wasn't looking any happier than she felt. Had he been hoping to be chosen for the team too? Probably. That boygod did not lack confidence. He also liked being the center of attention and didn't

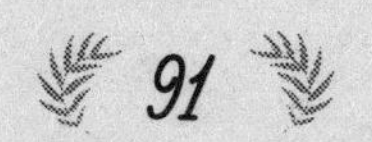

seem to care if it happened as the result of his bad behavior. Of course, this would've made him a risky choice for the team.

A hand touched Skade's shoulder. It was Balder's. Offering her a look of sympathy, he said, "Tough luck. I'm really sorry you're not on the main team." He yawned. "I'm glad you're coming to Jotunheim with us, though. Your and Angerboda's inside knowledge of the slopes will be a big help."

"We'll do our best," she replied, giving him a small smile.

When Balder yawned again, Skade tilted her head and studied him with concern. "You okay? I mean, you've been yawning a lot lately. You were doing it in history class today too." She was almost glad to have something else to worry about besides how upset she felt, even if only for a minute.

"Huh?" Balder said. "Oh, yeah." He yawned again. "Well, truth is, I haven't been getting much sleep the past few days. I've been having the weirdest dreams. Nightmares, really." He yawned again super big, just like Mr. Sturluson was famous for doing. Thinking of that teacher reminded Skade of his scolding words earlier that day. Which she didn't want to think about.

"Nightmares? What kind?" Thor asked, overhearing.

"Creepy stuff. Take last night, for example. Dreamed I was in Jotunheim, trapped inside a ring of skis that some frost giants had stuck on end in the snow around me like some kind of fence or jail bars," Balder said. "And another night I dreamed that giants had baked me into a humongous pie. I was getting exhausted swimming in berry juice, but I couldn't escape. Meanwhile, my giant captors were looking hungrier and hungrier. They were smacking their lips and chanting, 'Let's all try . . . some Balder-berry pie.'" With that, Balder gave a huge yawn, stretching his arms overhead.

"Mmm. Pie," echoed Loki, who had just wandered

over. He was always hungry, it seemed, and any discussion that involved food interested him. "So what finally happened? In your pie dream, I mean."

"Nothing. Right when the giants opened their mouths wide and were about to eat me, I woke up." Balder shuddered.

Skade did too. Most every frost giant she knew was suspicious of anyone from another world and would gladly do them mischief if given half a chance.

Balder yawned again and then slumped to sit in a chair at a nearby table. His head dropped, and he rested his chin on his fist on the tabletop. "That's how it always happens in the nightmares I've been having. Before I drown or fall into an enormous beehive or something awful like that, I wake up with a jolt. Then I'm tired all the next day," he added sleepily.

A strange fear for Balder's well-being prickled the back of Skade's neck. "Weird coincidence that you've been dreaming of frost giants, and then frost giants suddenly show up here at AA this afternoon to invite us to Jotunheim, don't you think?"

Balder sat up straighter. Thor, Loki, and everyone who had been listening in on their conversation leaned in to hear more. "Yeah, come to think of it, all my bad dreams have to do with giants causing me trouble. What do you think it means?"

"Maybe your dreams are some kind of prophecy?" said Thor. "We should go tell Odin and Ms. Frigg about them and see what they think." Pulling Balder to stand, the superstrong Thor half-dragged him over to the coprincipals across the room to do just that while Skade, Loki, and some other students followed.

They listened again as Balder described his troubling dreams to both Odin and Ms. Frigg. "You were right to come to us with this news. It's very worrisome," Odin said afterward. "As a boygod, you are destined to live forever young. Unless you are *purposely* killed."

Ms. Frigg's hand flew to her cheek and she gasped in

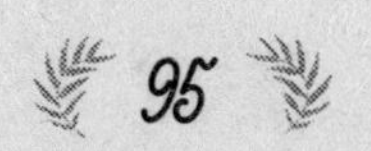

horror. "But who or what in the worlds would ever do such a thing? Everyone adores our sweet Balder!" Students who had collected around them nodded in agreement.

"Maybe Balder should be taken off the team," Loki suggested to Ms. Frigg. "For his own safety, of course. I volunteer myself to take his place," he added hopefully.

Balder grinned and elbowed him, not taking offense. "You crack me up. Always the jokey Loki!"

However, then Balder's forehead wrinkled with worry as he turned toward Odin again. "You won't count me out of the competition because of my nightmares, will you?"

"Nightmares very often do portend injury or trouble of some sort," said Odin, tapping his chin with a finger and appearing thoughtful.

"But it wouldn't be fair to take him out of the ski games due to a few nightmares," insisted Skade. Despite her concern for Balder, she knew how *she'd* feel if she had a solid spot on the team, then was told she couldn't participate after all because of some crazy dreams.

Just then Ms. Frigg snapped her fingers. "I have an idea. We'll simply demand a promise from every dangerous object or being in the nine worlds not to do Balder any harm."

"Is that possible?" asked Njord. "The games begin the day after tomorrow. How can we send a message out to all harmful things everywhere and get them to swear an oath not to harm Balder in just one day?"

Until that moment Skade hadn't even noticed that Njord had joined the group. Though she'd been wondering the exact same thing, she'd never admit that to him since she'd begun to dislike him so much.

However, Loki nodded at the boygod in agreement. "Good point." Then he helpfully began counting off the many possible sources of harm that could do Balder in and that would therefore need to quickly make a promise not to. "Water could drown him. Boulders could fall on him. A bear could eat him. And what about poisonous plants, insects, diseases . . . ?"

"Yikes! Enough," said Balder, going a little pale.

Skade rolled her eyes. "Yeah, we get the idea, Loki. Thanks a lot."

"The matter is settled!" Odin announced boldly, sending Ms. Frigg a nod. "We'll send my ravens out on swift wings to gather all required oaths." With that, he clapped his hands twice, calling out, "Hugin! Munin! Come!"

His voice hadn't seemed loud enough to reach beyond the cafeteria walls. But somehow, seconds later, his two large black ravens swooped inside through one of the Valhallateria's high windows. *Flap! Flap!* The pair landed to perch on each of Odin's shoulders.

He began stroking their feathers as he spoke to them. "Hugin and Munin, I command you to fly forth and visit anything in our nine worlds that is capable of causing death or illness. From each such being or object, you must secure a promise to do no harm to the boygod Balder. One oath per species will suffice. For instance, no need to make *every* thorn swear—a single oath from a single thorn not to prick will do the trick. This feat must be accomplished by daybreak on Saturday before the ski games begin in Jotunheim. Keep in mind that's the day after tomorrow."

Normally ravens only flew by day, but Odin's were magical and would be well able to carry out his bidding in daylight or darkness. The feathered pair nodded in unison, and from their sharp beaks came cries that indicated their understanding of the important assignment they'd been tasked with. *Caw! Caw!* Rising, they spiraled overhead a few times before flapping out via the same high window they'd entered through moments earlier.

Almost as if their departure had been some sort of signal, a dozen cafeteria ladies known as Valkyries now swarmed out of the kitchen to circulate among the dining tables. Each of them carried a six-foot-wide tray balanced on one hand containing heaping plates of food. The ladies wore gleaming metal helmets, and across their chests were breastplates with rows of loops down the front that held silver spoons and knives and fresh rolled-up napkins. It was dinnertime!

Hungry students scrambled to take seats at the various tables. Before Skade could join her friends at one of them, Odin stopped her with a hand on her shoulder. She turned toward him. The usual black patch covered one of his eyes. But his other eye—a clear, intelligent blue one—was fixed on her.

"I suppose you're wondering why you aren't on the main team. I know you must be disappointed," he remarked.

Startled, Skade gulped and looked away, momentarily unable to find her tongue. But she recovered quickly. "Was it because of my grade in Norse History? Thing is, I've been working on my dancing, and . . ."

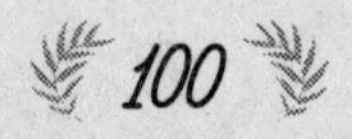

Odin crossed his muscular arms. "I'm sorry, but as it stands now your history grade is below average. Mr. Sturluson felt that your attitude needs work too. I'd have to agree. Ms. Frigg and I saw you arguing with Angerboda on the ski slopes this afternoon. She tried to hug you, yet your first reaction was to pull away."

Skade sighed. "We don't get along all that well." She knew she wasn't helping her chances (if she actually had any right now) by confirming what Odin had said.

"That's not the kind of good sportsmanship we hope to model in Jotunheim this weekend," Odin told her in a gently chiding voice. "Since we decided to send our team out first thing tomorrow morning to allow for ski practice time in Jotunheim, we had to base our nine selections on information available to us today. So I'm afraid those black marks counted against you." Odin cocked his head at her, his single good eye seeming to see deep inside her thoughts.

Suddenly she found herself blurting out her feelings

to him. "I just . . . It's so frustrating not to make the main team. Everyone expected me to."

Odin nodded. "No one doubts that you're a superb skier. That's part of the reason you were made alternate, despite the marks against you. We hope you'll provide advice to your teammates. And inspire confidence." He turned to go.

"Well, I don't feel very confident right now," Skade murmured to herself.

Overhearing her, Odin turned back her way. He regarded her keenly again. "You know, after I lost my eye, many of Asgard's enemies hoped it would make me weak. That it meant our world might be easily defeated. I could have given up, let them conquer our villages, and proven them right. Instead, I put on a fierce-looking eye patch and spoke to them with bold courage.

"Guess what. Every time I faced down a fear, no matter how big or small, I gained courage and strength. The more confident I acted, the more confident I felt. Half of being confident is simply *acting* confident," he said, his blue eye gleaming. "Other worlds believed what they saw. And what they saw in me was a confident leader. And what I see in you is the same. Our ski team needs you. Needs your confidence. Confidence is key. Never forget that. Don't let us down."

Skade gulped. "I'll try not to."

Odin's words stayed with her throughout dinner. If she didn't feel confident at times, could she pretend to? Then maybe her confidence would become real like Odin's had. She was still wondering if she could do what Odin expected of her when she stepped outside with her podmates to head for Vingolf dorm.

Brrr. She shivered in the cold air and wrapped herself in her cloak more tightly. It was dark now, and a light snow was swirling. Abruptly, a flapping sound reached her ears.

"Look!" Sif called out. She pointed upward. Perhaps having already secured oaths from potential sources of harm close to the Valhallateria, Odin's two ravens were now winging off to secure promises from beings and objects farther away. Skade's mind boggled at the enormity of their task. Water, stone, fire, diseases, metals, berries, trees, animals. The list was seemingly endless! Yet oaths would have to be exacted from all.

The effort would be worth it, though. She truly was glad that a protective shield was being woven around Balder. And not just so that AA could successfully compete in the games. But also because he was the nicest boygod she knew!

6
Beanies

BY FRIDAY MORNING AFTER BREAKFAST, ALL nine ski team members plus Skade had packed their belongings into one bag each. (Except for Freya, who, as the girlgoddess of beauty, needed *two* bags to hold all her extra clothes and accessories.)

First off, they planned to travel via a system of magical slides within AA's Heartwood Library. Then they'd walk the rest of the way to Jotunheim. This meant they'd be carrying their skis as well as their bags, which was quite an armload. They'd likely be exhausted by the time they arrived at the ski games, Skade realized as she juggled her stuff. Freya more than anyone.

When they gathered outside on a path halfway between the boys' and girls' dorms, Odin and a cheering group of AA students and teachers were there to see them off. Including Sif and Idun.

Odin spread his arms wide, beaming at them. "Team Asgard! We here at the academy wish you a swift and safe journey to Jotunheim this morning," he began in his powerful voice. "Tomorrow, Ratatosk and his message acorns, as well as Nidhogg the dragon to the south and the eagle-eyed eagle to the north, will all help spread news of how the ski games are progressing."

He paused a moment to adjust his eye patch, which had slid down a little, before going on. "I'll be checking up on you with my Eye telescope from time to time, though I won't interfere unless you've encountered the rare situation I feel you aren't capable of handling.

There is great excitement for this event throughout the worlds. I bid you good luck and know that you will make us proud. Which means play fair, make friends, and excel on the ski slopes!"

A thrill shot through Skade, lifting her spirits as more loud cheers went up. Even though she wouldn't get to compete, she *was* proud to be going to the games.

She and her teammates had bent to grab their luggage, planning to troop down the fernway toward the library when a voice called out. They turned to see Ms. Frigg hurrying toward them. "Wait! I'm so glad I caught you before you left. I've made gifts for the ten of you," she told them, smiling big.

Ymir's knuckles! Skade and the other students on the team froze in place. Their eyes grew big and maybe even a little worried. Because although all of Asgard adored Ms. Frigg and cherished her gifts, they were kind of famous for being . . . *quirky*. Right now her teammates were probably all recalling some of the gifts

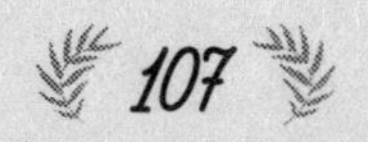

Ms. Frigg had bestowed in the past, Skade figured. For instance, the vest she'd knitted for the school security guard, Heimdall. It had pink tassels all over it. Sooo *not* him. And the six-toed, flowered socks she'd knitted for Odin. *Yikes!*

The items Ms. Frigg held out to them now were made of a beautiful, strong yarn she was famous for spinning. But what were they? Skade wondered.

Smiling in delight, Ms. Frigg distributed her newest gifts among the team members. Then, taking a step back, she clasped her hands together. "Guess what they are!"

All ten of them examined their identical knitted gifts and then glanced at one another uncertainly. Unwilling to risk a guess that might hurt Ms. Frigg's feelings, no one spoke up.

Skade would bet that not even Odin, nor any of the teachers and students in the crowd, had the faintest idea about what these gifts were meant to be. To her, they

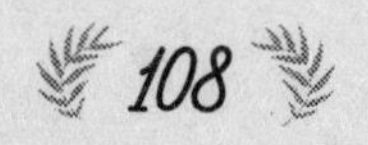

looked like bowls with two brown-fingered hands growing like roots from their bottoms. Surely, that couldn't be right.

Before anyone had to guess, Ms. Frigg gleefully provided the answer. "They're reindeer antler beanies! To protect you, warm you, and bring you luck in Jotunheim."

What they would not do was inspire confidence, though, thought Skade. Hers took a nosedive as she stared at the beanie she held. Because these beanies were *goofy*. They would make the AA team members look weak to the other competitors. Their team was going to get teased if they wore the beanies. To increase their chances of winning, they needed to appear as fierce to the other teams in Jotunheim as Odin's eye patch had made him to Asgard's enemies. The stronger they looked, the more self-assured they'd feel. Which would help them to perform at their very best, right?

However, neither she nor anyone else on her team

wanted to tell Ms. Frigg any of this. So instead, they all thanked her and quickly folded the beanies away in their pockets for "safekeeping." Waving goodbye, the team moved off through the golden forest toward the school library.

Walking along in the cold, crisp air, Skade's mood soon lightened again. She loved winter. Which was a good thing since it often snowed in eight of the Norse worlds. Only the terrible world of Muspelheim was said to be fiery hot and completely snowless. It was two rings below Asgard, but only one ring below Jotunheim. She'd never met an eyewitness who'd actually ever seen the land of the fire giants, though.

The team wove silently through tall blue spruces, rowan trees with red berries, and past holly bushes. Although there were many kinds of trees growing atop Yggdrasil's enormous branches, they were like tiny twigs compared to Yggdrasil itself. The huge ash tree was like a gigantic, leafy umbrella with three humongous roots.

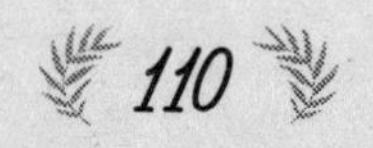

Its trunk was so big that Skade and her podmates figured it would take someone an entire lifetime to walk all the way around it!

"This stuff is heavy," Freya remarked after a bit, shifting the bags and skis she carried. "How about if I use my cart to fly to Jotunheim ahead of you guys? I can take all the ski equipment, plus all of our bags."

Everyone was in favor of this idea. So once they reached a clearing, Freya quickly pulled her colorful cat's-eye marble from its fist-size pouch, which hung from one of her necklaces. The marble had been a gift on her twelfth birthday from her twin brother, Frey, Skade knew.

Freya tossed it high. *Plink!* The marble landed on the snowy ground a short distance from the group. Instantly it transformed into two pony-size gray tabby cats, both hitched to pull a red cart. *Meow! Meow!*

After they all gratefully piled their skis and bags into the kittycart, Freya stepped inside and took its reins in

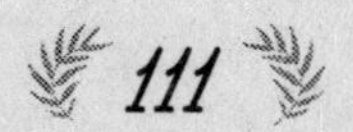

her hands. “Looks like I’ve got room for one passenger,” she said after surveying the cart’s load. “It would help to have someone with me who knows the way to Jotunheim.”

She smiled at Skade in invitation, but before Skade could make a move, Angerboda called out, “Sure, I’ll go with you!” And she hopped into the cart beside Freya.

This was not at all how either Skade or Freya would have preferred things to go, of course. But after throwing Skade an apologetic glance, Freya called out to her magical cats. “Fly, kitty, kitty!” In a flash, she and Angerboda were off in the cart, zooming through the air in the direction of Jotunheim.

That left Skade and the other seven team members, Balder, Honir, Njord, Thor, Yanis, Malfrid, and Ull, to continue making their way to the library on foot. They soon entered a dense grove of thin birch trees, which led them right up to Yggdrasil’s trunk.

Each student used a fingertip to trace the words

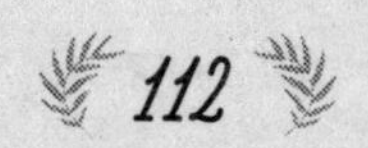

“Knowledge is power” on one of their palms. Then they stepped forward, standing shoulder to shoulder while facing the tree with their noses and toes pressed against its bark.

Whoosh! Instantly the group found itself pulled inside to a hollowed-out space in the very center of the tree’s trunk. It took powerful magic to transport an entire team of students through tree bark all the way into the library hidden deep within the center of this tree. Yggdrasil magic!

7
To Totunheim

THE LIBRARY'S CURVED INNER WALLS WERE lined with shelves of books filled with writing in the form of symbols called runes. These shelves extended as far downward as the eye could see. There were ladders on wheels that followed tracks here and there along the shelves. By climbing from one ladder to another, all the floors and their books could be reached.

A sign nearby read:

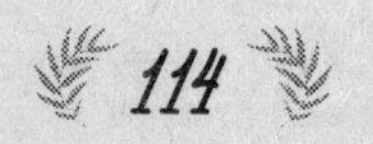

Knowledge Is Power

Together, the eight students now stood on a round wooden floor. Approximately two hundred feet across, it had a large hole in its center, through which they could see numerous floors below them with similar holes. Several transparent tubular travel slides that ranged from about one to four feet in diameter corkscrewed up through the holes from deep below.

A column of bright blue water shot through one of the tubular slides to bubble up in a tall spout at eye level. Atop the spout a man's head spun around and around. It was Mimir, the very brilliant *head* librarian!

"Welcome!" he greeted Skade and the others. Then he gestured toward a group of four-foot-wide tubes nearby. "I understand you are off to ski in Jotunheim. Any of these water slides will take you close to there. They all end in the Spring of Mimir, on the second world ring between Jotunheim and Darkalfheim."

When the librarian bobbed his head, an assistant named Gullveig (who used to be Freya's childhood nanny in Vanaheim) pushed a green wall switch. The water in those spouts, which had been flowing upward, immediately reversed to flow downward. One after the other, the students each jumped into a separate tube.

Skade went first, always eager for action. And besides, she'd taken a slide down to Jotunheim before, so she knew how much fun it could be. Caught in the downward flow, she shouted "Woo-hoo!" Swiftly she was whirled through the maze of transparent water slides, descending from floor to floor.

Over in other tubes she caught sight of her friends and waved as she swooshed down, down, down. Purposely, she did somersaults and funny poses inside her tube, making her teammates giggle. To go faster, she bodysurfed at times, or hugged her knees to her chest to tumble through the tube like a spinning top.

Often on her downward journey things became

a blur outside her tube, but then some strange curiosity would pop into view. Like the glowing eyes that peeked out of a strange painting of salmon displayed on one shelf, for example. On another, a fanciful army of insects marched along. Snowflakes with real faces twirled out from among the pages of a book on yet another shelf, singing silly rhyming songs. Skade caught part of a lyric as she slid by:

"We love to sparkle in the sun.
Drifting down is so much fun.
Until we melt, and then we're done!"

Abruptly their trips came to an end when the eight students shot out of the tubes. *Splash! Splash! Splash! Splash! Splash! Splash! Splash! Splash!* They landed sitting in the Spring of Mimir, the bubbling pool that nourished one of Yggdrasil's three great roots.

"Brr! We're all wet and it's starting to snow. We're

going to freeze to death!" exclaimed Ull. As the boygod of snow, he would know about such things. However, there was one thing he didn't know that Skade did.

"Don't worry. The waters of this spring are charmed," she told him. Grabbing onto a clump of bilberry bushes growing on the bank, she pulled herself out of the spring. Then she reached back to help the others out as well. Like magic, each of them immediately became totally dry once their boots touched land.

Snow-covered mountains stood to their left in the distance. Caves loomed to their right. Carved across the side of a craggy black peak among those caves were the words DARKALFHEIM: KEEP OUT!

Skade grinned, rolling her eyes at the peak. "Dwarfs. So welcoming, right?" The rest of the team laughed, knowing that the grumpy dwarfs in those caves chose to live there for a reason. They were secretive about their jewelry-making skills and didn't want anyone to copy from them. Or even worse, to steal their hoard of gold! Once, they'd actually stolen Freya's jewel, Brising, though. She'd bravely ignored the warning on the peak, gone to their caves, and reclaimed it. And she'd even returned a second time, with Sif. They'd spied on Loki after he cut off Sif's magical golden hair and was forced to visit the dwarfs to ask for replacement hair and other gifts for the gods.

"Jotunheim's this way," said Skade. "C'mon, follow me." Turning her back on the caves, she headed for the snow-capped mountains. As they all walked along, they chatted among themselves, growing more and more excited about the upcoming games.

"Ow. My boots are pinching my little toes," Njord complained after walking on the trail awhile. "My old ones wore out, so I bought these yesterday at Midgard Mall. I haven't broken them in yet."

"You can switch to another pair when we get to Jotunheim," said Skade. "It's not that much farther, and Freya will have all your stuff there."

"But I only brought one pair. That's all I own," Njord informed her.

"You only own *one* pair of boots?" Skade echoed in shock, glancing back at him.

"What's wrong with that?" asked Ull. "I only own one pair."

"Me too." "Same here." "So do I," admitted the other three boys.

"I own four pairs," piped up Yanis.

"I own five," said Malfrid. They were walking directly behind Skade. The three of them were the only girls in the group now, since Freya and Angerboda had taken the kittycart.

The boys looked stunned at this information. "Howw manee d'yoo own?" Balder ask-yawned Skade.

"Counting the pair I'm wearing? Thirteen," Skade replied easily.

The boys all gasped.

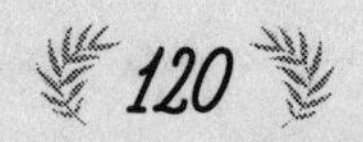

"That's crazy!" said Thor. "You girls only have two feet. Why so many boots?"

"You're right. We are crazy," Skade agreed, turning to grin back at Yanis and Malfrid. "Crazy about boots, that is."

"Yeah," said Yanis, giggling and high-fiving her.

"Each pair I own has pros and cons but is special in its own way," added Malfrid.

"Exactly!" Skade nodded in complete understanding. "I have speedy boots, lightweight boots, knee-highs, shorties, faux fur–lined ankle boots, and so on."

"Oh brother," said Njord, rolling his eyes.

"All the girls I know have at least two pairs," said Yanis.

"Uh-huh," said Malfrid. "Because what if your boots get wet? You need a dry pair."

"That's a good point," said Balder. "I usually wind up walking around in wet boots half the time. Maybe these girls have the right idea."

The three girls smiled at him. There was a reason everyone liked Balder. He really was super-duper nice!

Just then, they came to a fork in the snowy trail they were following. Whenever that happened, Skade's companions looked to her for instruction. "This way," she said, forging onward.

"I'm glad you're on the team," Balder said when they wound up walking side by side.

"Sort of on the team, you mean," said Skade. "I'm only the alternate."

Balder shook his head. "You're an important member. And it's great having you along. Since you and Angerboda are both from Jotunheim, you'll be able to give us insider tips. So we don't mistakenly do things that giants consider bad manners and stuff like that."

Nearby, Skade felt Njord staring at them, listening. When she looked over at him, however, he glanced away. What was up with that guy, anyway?

As she had anticipated, their group arrived at

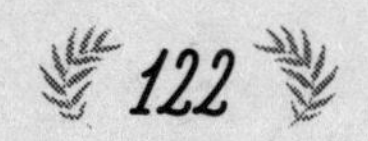

Jotunheim around noon. By now, she noticed that Njord was definitely limping. "I'd offer to lend you a pair of my boots, but I don't think they'd fit you," she told him kindly. As soon as the words were out of her mouth, she braced for a snarky comeback.

But instead of saying something like *Why would I want to wear your stinky boots?* he merely replied, "That's okay. Mine should be broken in by tomorrow." He actually appeared confused and a little embarrassed by her kindness, probably because he'd never been very nice to her.

"Hey, there's Freya's kittycart," said Ull, pointing. "Minus the kitties. She must've plinked them back into their marble after they landed."

Skade followed his finger. Angerboda was inside the cart. She was digging through her belongings and looked up when the rest of the team reached her. Immediately, everyone stormed the cart and began sorting through their bags for the snacks they'd brought, which they quickly gobbled down. They were eager to hit the slopes!

"Freya and I have already skied down a couple of runs," Angerboda said in greeting. "I came back to get my mittens and scarf. It's getting colder. Come on, I'll show you guys the way to the runs," she offered while everyone grabbed their skis.

When Skade started to follow with the others, though, Angerboda called back to her. "Hey, Skade. Could you take all of our stuff from the cart and stow it in the dorms? The rest of us need this afternoon for doing practice runs on the slopes before our big day tomorrow."

"Oh, um, sure. No problem." Although disappointed not to get to ski with the group now and a bit hurt to be singled out as less important, Skade couldn't really argue. Because what Angerboda suggested made sense. As alternate, Skade could spare the time to unload the cart more than any of the rest of them could.

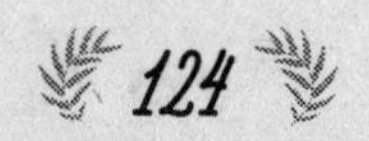

“Skrymir told us we’ll be staying in those igloos over there. They’re temporary, built just for us to use during the games,” Angerboda informed her. Skade looked in the direction she’d pointed to see two huge igloos built out of ice blocks. One igloo was marked BOYS and the other was marked GIRLS.

Skade turned back to the cart.

“Need any help?” Balder asked her. (Again, such a nice guy!)

“No, thanks, I can handle it,” she replied. “You guys take your skis and get going. I’ll join you when I’m done.” She was trying her hardest to appear okay about being left behind. This was partly so that Angerboda wouldn’t have the satisfaction of knowing she was making her squirm! But inside Skade felt sort of put-down and embarrassed. *Odin knows what’s best,* she reminded herself when she couldn’t quite squash the angry feelings inside her over not being on the main team. Still, telling herself that didn’t really make her feel better.

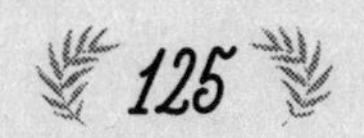

It would take six trips to get all their bags where they belonged, she estimated. She grabbed some of the boys' bags from the cart first and tromped in the direction of their igloo.

She'd only taken a few steps when a boygiant blocked her path. He stood five times her height and held a large, flat sheet of tree bark with a list of teams written on it. *Ugh.* It was Skrymir. He hadn't seen her on the wall the previous day during his visit to AA, she didn't think. But there could be no avoiding his notice now.

"World?" he asked her, not looking up from his list.

"Asgard," said Skade. She kept her head bent down and let her long hair, which she'd worn loose today, slide forward to shield her face. Fingers crossed he couldn't see her well enough to recognize her.

No such luck, though.

"Hey, don't I know you?" he asked, bending lower to see her face.

"Uh, maybe?" she mumbled.

Skrymir's eyes lit up with gleeful mischief. "Rabbit? It's you! Haven't seen you since last summer."

She groaned. "My name is *Skade.*" She'd been given the role of a frightened rabbit character in a play years ago in Jotunheim kindergarten summer camp. Unfortunately, he'd never forgotten.

"Sure, Scaredy-Rabbit, whatever you say. You're hopping—I mean, heading—the wrong way with those bags, though. Girls' igloo is over there," he informed her, pointing. "Inside there'll be a sign on the door of your team's sleeping unit."

She nodded to indicate the bags she was carrying. "I have some of the boys' stuff to stow first."

If he was curious to know why she was doing all the luggage delivery, he didn't ask. "Girls can't go inside the boys' igloo," he informed her. "Just stack their bags in the mudroom right inside the front door. The boys on your team can take their stuff to the unit they'll all share in the igloo later on."

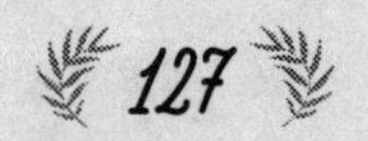

After Skade supplied him with all the names on her team, he checked them off. "Hey, some guy named Ull is listed as captain and you're listed as the alternate. Is that a mistake?"

She gritted her teeth, then made herself admit the truth. "No."

Skrymir looked stunned by this information and not altogether happy about it either. That was odd. Usually, he'd be the first to tease her about something like this. Quickly she headed for the boys' igloo before he could ask further questions her about her position on the team.

She stowed the boys' stuff in their mudroom as instructed. Then she went back and forth between Freya's cart and both dorms several more times until she eventually grabbed the last of the load and made for the girls' igloo. Inside it, nine areas called units had been zoned off. One for each group of girls on each ski team. Even those competitors who lived in Jotunheim were being asked to stay in the temporary igloos it seemed.

On her final return to the cart for her skis before going to find her friends, she was glad to see that Skrymir was distracted by a team of giants newly arrived for the games. She'd never seen giants like these before. They had small, mean orange eyes and fiery red hair.

"Muspelheim. I'm team captain," announced a boy-giant who stood a foot taller than the rest. Skade's eyes went wide. That meant these had to be fire giants! No one she knew had ever met a fire giant before. Because, of course, the world of Muspelheim had disobeyed Odin by not sending any students to AA.

As Skrymir checked off the names of each fire giant team member, she walked past, studying them while pretending not to. Their team was all boys. Not a single girl. Looked like the Muspelheim sleeping zone in the girls' igloo would remain empty.

Noticing that their captain carried a strange-looking red sword, Skade drew in a sharp breath. This had to be Surt, the fire giant Loki had admired! His team was hanging on his every word, obviously in awe of him. He looked cocky and smirky, like he would cut you down if you ever dared speak to him. It was well-known that he often bragged (even once to Odin himself!) that his sword was so powerful, it could destroy all the worlds.

Her head spinning now, Skade scurried to the kitty-cart. There was still plenty of time to hit the slopes, thankfully. She grabbed her skis and hurried off to enjoy some runs. *Sweet!*

8
Tricks

AFTER SEVERAL HOURS OF FRESH AIR AND sunshine on the slopes, Skade came across Freya. "Guess what? Surt's here!" she told her friend right away.

Freya's blue eyes went wide with concern. "Surt the fire giant?" She glanced this way and that as if to spot him. "Where? Is he as scary-looking as they say?"

Skade nodded downhill to where he and some other members of his team were skiing. "You be the judge. He's right over there."

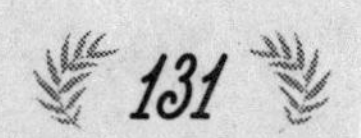

Looking at the fire giants, she and Freya both shivered. "Definitely scary," they murmured at the same time. Their whole team wore bright red sweaters and boots decorated with yellow flames. As the captain, Surt's had yellow *and* orange flames. These bold outfits were obviously meant to intimidate. Plus, he was carrying his sword while skiing. Which was not only weird—it was dangerous!

"Too bad we didn't have more time to get ready for this competition. I could've made matching outfits for *our* team," Freya said wistfully.

"Hmm. I wonder if Asgard was the last team to be invited. On purpose," mused Skade.

"To give us less time to prepare, you mean?" Freya considered the idea. "Sadly, that sounds like something the frost giants might do." Then, obviously recalling that Skade was from Jotunheim, she hurriedly added, "No offense."

"None taken. What you said is true," said Skade.

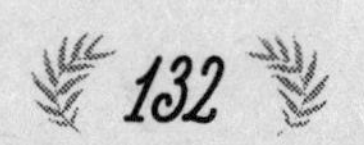

She had braided her hair before hitting the slopes and now flipped the single braid over one shoulder to hang at her back. "We'll just have to make the best of it. Someone had to be last to hear, after all. And we'll still win." *Hmm.* Saying that last bit had actually made her feel a tingle of her old confidence. And it wasn't *pretend* confidence either!

Although frost giants were troublemakers, fire giants were a different story. They were pure *evil.* At Asgard Academy, the students had all learned that Surt and his friends would be the force behind Ragnarok, if it ever came about. Destroying Yggdrasil and all the worlds just so they could become the bosses of whatever would be left was definitely an evil plan. This competition was supposed to be about making friends. At least partly. But could anyone make friends with evil?

Why had the fire giants decided to attend this competition? Skade wondered. If she hadn't been afraid of being overheard by others, she might have asked for

Freya's thoughts on the matter. But really, neither of them could possibly know the reason. And the slopes were calling to them. So they took off in the opposite direction of the fire giants, skiing side by side.

Whee! Both girlgoddesses were soon happily zooming down one run after another. They all had fun names, such as Don't Look Down, Beary Steep, and even Yikes. Each was marked with a colored sign to indicate its level of difficulty. Ski runs marked with a green sign were the easiest, wide with gentle slopes. Blue runs got a little harder. Black ones became still more challenging. But any run with two black diamonds on its sign could mean trouble even for experienced skiers like Freya and Skade. Those were steep, narrow, and icy, which meant you had to make tight, fast turns. And they could be dotted with hazards you had to dodge, such as rocks, trees, and cliffs.

Toward the end of the day, after Skade had skied many of the slopes either alone or with Freya, the two of them met up with Angerboda, Malfrid, and Yanis.

"Isn't this fun?" Yanis exclaimed. In typical light-elf fashion, she was wriggling and bouncing with joy. She'd probably be twirling around and doing little dance steps too, if she weren't on skis right now!

Malfrid giggled. Angerboda was smiling a rare smile as well. However, Skade didn't trust *her* smile. And she knew she'd been smart not to when Angerboda suggested, "Let's all go do the Helrun."

Huh? That girlgiant knew the trouble Skade had had while skiing that run years ago and had probably guessed (correctly!) that she was nervous of trying it again.

"Helrun is a double black diamond, right?" Freya said doubtfully. She shook her head, causing her hair, which she'd done up in two blond braids, to sway from side to side. "I'm too tired for that one right now. I need to save some energy for the competition tomorrow."

Thank goodness, thought Skade in relief.

"How about you, Skade?" asked Angerboda, practically snickering.

Skade stiffened. Would it be fun to roll head over skis all the way to the bottom of Helrun as everyone looked on? Ha! But if Angerboda guessed how afraid she still was of that run, she might earn some new nicknames in addition to Rabbit. And those nicknames might be Chicken and Fraidy-Cat. If only Odin and Ms. Frigg knew this mean, taunting side of Angerboda, they'd never have considered her for the team no matter how good a skier she was.

But then, remembering Odin's words to her, Skade straightened. *Half of being confident is simply* acting *confident.* So even though Angerboda's remarks had hit their target, Skade stuck out her chin, took a deep breath, and calmly replied, "Sure, let's do it."

Angerboda's smile wobbled in disappointed surprise. She'd hoped to upset Skade and punch holes in her confidence. *Too bad for her!*

Before Angerboda could take her up on her offer, however, the boys from their team—Thor, Njord, Honir,

Ull, and Balder—skied over. "There's a girls-only aerial ski tricks competition on one of the ski jumps in five minutes," Balder announced to them. "It's to choose competitors for one of the three main events tomorrow."

Skade perked up, her eyebrows arching with interest. "Aerial ski tricks?"

"Yeah," Balder answered. "C'mon! Girls on any of the teams can try out. Including alternates, Skade!"

Hooray! Not only did this sound like *true* fun, but it would also save her from having to ski that devilish Helrun. As excitement filled her, Skade's eyes flew over the groups of students heading for this unexpected competition. Her gaze locked on Skrymir. He was looking her way, grinning secretively now. *Uh-oh.* What was that about?

"Count me in," said Angerboda. Her teammates all followed as she dug her poles into the snow and pushed off in the direction others were going.

"I didn't think the competitions were supposed to

start till tomorrow," said Freya as they all made their way to the appropriate ski jump.

"The frost giants just announced this event an hour ago to all the team captains," said Thor. The girls looked over at Ull, the AA captain, for information.

"These'll just be tryouts," he informed them, leaning both wrists atop his ski poles. "The three best girl skiers from today's tryouts are supposed to each choose a boy partner from any team later for a pairs event tomorrow. We're not sure on how that choosing part's going to work yet."

Njord jumped in. "Also, didn't you tell me that the goal at tomorrow's games is for the three pairs of partners to vie to win an aerial ski tricks competition?"

Ull nodded. "Yeah. It'll be one of the three main events Saturday."

Whoa! This was her chance to become part of the team for real, thought Skade. Even though alternates were allowed to compete in this one event, she could bet Angerboda was hoping Skade would decide not to. As if!

Minutes later, Skade, Yanis, Angerboda, Freya, Malfrid, and other girls were riding upward in wooden gondolas whose outsides had been stenciled with white-painted snowflakes and reindeer designs. The gondolas took them to the top of a large snow-covered hill via a system of pulleys, to where the ski acrobatics tryouts would begin. A group of judges, with members from various worlds, instructed the competitors that each would have only one chance to perform and showcase their skills. No do-overs. *Gulp!*

By now a crowd had gathered to watch from a stand at the bottom of the ski jump. But the watchers wouldn't make Skade feel a bit nervous when her turn came. It was easy to be confident about something you knew you excelled at. She'd been performing aerial ski tricks for years and had won lots of contest ribbons in such events.

Aerial ski tricks involved four main actions. First, you

poised on a high ramp called an inrun. Then you jumped off the edge of an area called a takeoff table. Next came your flight, which was her favorite part because she got to sail through the air like a bird, doing flips, twists, and more. And finally, there was the landing. In summer, the sun could turn the landing area into hard-packed ice. But in winter, the landing area was often covered in fluffy snow called powder, like now. Compared to landing on solid ice, powder was less jarring. Which made it more fun to ski on.

The girls all drew lengths of straw to determine the order in which they would jump. Skade drew the longest straw, so she would be last, behind all the other girls, including her AA teammates. Competitors and spectators alike yelled encouragement to each new performer that tried out with calls such as "More air!" and "Go for greatness!"

A warm feeling of camaraderie filled Skade as she joined the cheering. They weren't just rooting for their

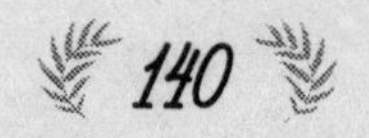

own teams. They were encouraging *everyone* to do well. Which was great sportsmanship!

When it was finally her turn to compete, Skade stepped onto the inrun. She leaned forward, causing her skis to begin gliding down the smooth, icy slope ahead. As she neared the takeoff point, she picked up speed. Then she launched into the air. She was practically flying!

No poles were used in these jumps, so her hands were free. Nimbly, she curled her body forward, tucking her hands under the bend of her knees. High in the air, she flipped herself backward, tumbling head over skis three times while twisting in a sideways tornado-like spin. When she came out of her last flip, she straightened. Skis-down now, she prepared to land with one ski tip placed slightly in front of the other and knees flexed.

Touchdown! She nailed it—a perfect landing! As she skied to a stop across the fluffy snow, she raised both arms high in a V for victory. She knew her super-duper triple jump had been flawless, and she'd aced her landing. All around her, loud cheers sounded.

By the time the judges chose the winners, it was nearly dusk. Three were declared, based on the distance and style of their jumps—a Midgardian human girl named Katrina and a freckled girl from Vanaheim named Olga. And Skade! The judges informed competitors and spectators alike that the three winners would be asked to choose partners after dinner tonight.

"Pick me! Pick me!" boys from various teams immediately called out. They waved and did somersaults and silly poses, flexing their muscles in hopes of influencing the three winning girls' choices of partners. In Skade's humble opinion, the boys from Asgard were the best aerial jumpers, so she'd probably pick one of them as a partner.

Soon everyone began making their way off the slopes. As night came on, the snow appeared to turn a sparkling soft-blue color. Skade glanced up. Above them, Nott was driving her chariot into the sky. Earlier, she'd been one of the judges. But now she was tossing stars and a dark veil of night out across the heavens as she flew ever higher.

What a great day this turned out to be! Skade thought as she and the other four AA girls set off for their igloo. She'd never anticipated she'd get to compete in an event!

"Fantastic jump, Skade! Who are you going to partner with for tomorrow's competition?" Malfrid asked as they all slowly skied in the direction everyone was going.

"Well, I haven't really—" began Skade.

"Who cares? I'm hungry. Let's skip the igloo for now and go get some dinner," Angerboda butted in to say. She was obviously not interested in discussing Skade's success and partner-choosing plans. Probably because Angerboda had been chosen fourth—an alternate in the aerial ski tricks tryouts, which had to annoy her to no end. In fact, she'd likely decided it was Skade's fault she'd been edged out of the first three places. Whatever!

Since they were all hungry, they picked up their pace, swerving in the direction of the cafeteria. When Skade's stomach growled a moment later, she grinned. "Obviously, I'm kind of starving too. Good thing we're off to the Gruntery!"

Bursts of laughter escaped Freya and the giggly Yanis and Malfrid, who were skiing just ahead of Angerboda and her. "The Gruntery?" the three girls chorused.

"Yeah. That's the name of the Jotunheim school cafeteria," Angerboda informed them. After a few minutes of skiing in silence, she added, "So what? It's not funny."

"We're used to it," Skade said to her. "But I guess that name would sound weird to anyone hearing it for the first time." As they reached the large wood-built cafeteria, the AA boys caught up to them. After they all removed their skis and set them in special built-in ski racks next to the Gruntery, Skade walked over and grabbed one of the cafeteria's iron door handles. "This

place is called the Gruntery for a reason," she told the others. "You'll see."

"The Gruntery?" some of the boys repeated, but she didn't bother to explain. They'd figure it out soon enough.

After entering the cafeteria, the ten of them passed three very long dining tables. Each consisted of a series of rectangular tabletops that were actually flat, smooth slabs of stone set end to end so that they ran the length of the room. Strong, thick wooden posts supported these tabletops. And dozens and dozens of tree stumps, each cut to about two feet in height, sat on the floor around each table, serving as stools for diners. At one end of the room there was a large stage that was used for school plays, speeches, and ceremonies.

Right away, Angerboda and Skade led the other eight Asgard Academy students toward the open firepit at the center of the Gruntery. There they found several large black iron cauldrons full of a bubbling stew. Ladles

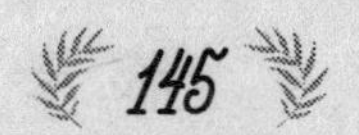

hung from the cauldrons' sides, and bowls, mugs, and pitchers were stacked on a low wall that surrounded the firepit. Teams from the various worlds had begun to gather there to fill bowls with stew and afterward wander over to the tables to eat. Dogs roamed freely throughout the cafeteria. Some were sleeping on the stone floor near the firepit to stay warm.

"As you can see, there's stew for dinner tonight. Looks like it's our choice of veggie, chicken, or bean," Skade said, gesturing at each of the cauldrons in turn. And there's buttermilk in those pitchers to drink, so grab a mug."

"What? No *rabbit* stew?" teased a voice behind her. Skade looked over her shoulder to see Skrymir grinning at her.

"So? You'll survive without it," Angerboda told him gruffly. If she remembered that nickname, she hadn't let on. But just in case, Skade didn't explain Skrymir's comment. She didn't want anyone else to start teasing her too!

Ignoring Skrymir, Skade quickly filled a bowl and

a mug. "C'mon, let's get a table," she suggested to her teammates as soon as they'd gotten their food and drink. Leading the way, she motioned for them all to follow. Freya, Yanis, and Balder remained near the cauldrons, however, chatting with newcomers.

She overheard Balder asking a dwarf what his cave school at Darkalfheim was like. Freya was telling a Midgardian human girl about the powers of her magic jewel, Brising. And Yanis was showing a dance move to a frost girlgiant. Those three were like goodwill ambassadors for Asgard Academy, all busy making new friends from other worlds as they came by to dip out stew. If Odin was using his telescope to observe them right now, he must be so pleased.

Skade settled on a stool at one end of their chosen table. "Oof," Ull complained when he plopped down on one of the wooden stumps across the table from her. "These seats are not nearly as comfy as the ones at the Valhallateria."

Thor and Honir sat on either side of him. "At least they're the right height for us, though, instead of giant-size," said Thor. "Kind of surprised about that, since this is a school for giants."

"Yeah, out on the slopes today, some giants enlarged to their giant-size selves," Njord remarked as he sat by Skade, while Angerboda and Malfrid took the stools to the left of him. "In here, all of them shrank themselves, though."

Skade pointed her spoon toward a sign high on the wall, directing his attention there. Reciting what it said by memory, she said, "No giant-sizing allowed in the Gruntery."

She was about to explain further, but just then Freya and Yanis arrived at their table having torn themselves away from the new friends they'd been making over at the cauldrons. Skade reached for a roll as Freya sat diagonally across from her by Thor, while Yanis sat by Malfrid.

On top of each long table, at intervals of every

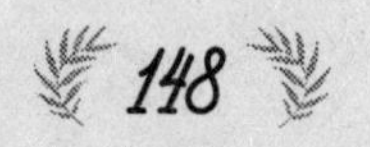

five feet or so, sat a cutting board with a large round of orange cheese, assorted knives and forks, and several loaves of fresh bread and butter. It was a feast!

While Skade buttered her roll, she went on to explain the reason for the sign. "I'll tell you why giant-sizing isn't allowed in here. Think about it. If we giants eat while we're large, we'd require bigger tables and stools, which is a waste of resources. Also it would take way more to feed us and more time for us to gobble stuff down."

"Makes sense," said Freya. After taking a bite of stew, she murmured, "Yum, this is good."

"Where are the cafeteria ladies?" asked Yanis, looking around.

"There aren't any. Jotunheim students take turns making food, setting tables, and doing cleanup," Angerboda informed her. Tonight, they'd placed bowls on the tables containing an assortment of raw fruits such as wild plums, apples, cherries, and pears, as well as vegetables such as cabbage, onions, leeks, turnips, and peas.

All around the AA team, other students began eating the minute they found tables and sat, obviously super hungry from skiing and traveling here earlier in the day. Soon loud smacking and slurping sounds started up—sounds that were *not* coming from their table. Skade's teammates looked around in surprise.

"What in Odin's name is that noise?" Thor asked quizzically.

"Sounds like we're at a pig farm," said Njord, his eyebrows rising.

Angerboda glared at him.

Grinning, Skade nodded to indicate some nearby tables, where giants were eating with their mouths full . . . and wide open. *Slurp, grunt, snort, burp.*

"Ugh." Freya wrinkled her nose at the way they were eating.

"What's up with the bad manners?" Balder asked, arriving just then to take a seat by Freya, across the table from Yanis.

"In Jotunheim, growling and grunting while eating is a way of showing appreciation for the food," Angerboda huffed. "It's *good* manners."

"I get it! So that must be why this cafeteria is called the *Grunt*ery!" said Honir.

Angerboda pointed the tip of her fork at him and nodded as if to say, *You're right.*

"Not sure I want to eat like that," murmured Yanis doubtfully. "Do I have to? I mean, is it actually considered rude here not to?"

"No, but it's kind of fun *snort* to use bad manners just this once, if you've never tried it before. You know *slurp,* like *grunty-grunt* I am doing right now *burp*," said Angerboda as she noisily gobbled her stew.

This made the others laugh. They began to copy her, giggling all the while. To Skade's surprise, a genuine smile lit Angerboda's face. But then, as if fearing that a true smile made her seem soft, she frowned again in her usual hard way and hunched over her bowl to

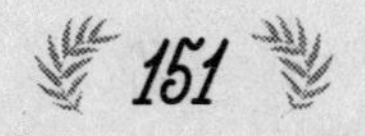

continue eating her stew and bread in earnest.

Skade grinned. "All this slurping does sound kinda icky now that I think about it. Fortunately, we were taught a quieter way to eat for when we venture out into other worlds."

When Freya reached over to stab some peas with the tip of her knife to add to her stew, they surprised her by boinging away. She drew back. "Whah?"

"Oops, forgot to mention that the vegetables here are picky about who eats them. You have to catch the ones you want to add to your stew. Approach them with self-assurance or they'll escape," instructed Skade.

"I don't know. I'd feel kind of bad eating food that doesn't want to be eaten," mused Balder.

Angerboda rolled her eyes. "Don't be silly. The veggies don't mind if you eat them. They just want you to prove you are determined enough and, you know, *worthy* of eating them."

To illustrate what Angerboda meant, Skade whipped

out her hand and snatched up some green peas still in their pods. "Gotcha!" she exclaimed. The pods wriggled within her closed fist, trying to escape, but she held on tight. "Stop fighting my will and become my meal. For I am Skade the strong and you are but weak, tasty peas." Hearing that, the peas seemed to decide that she was in fact worthy of eating them. They relaxed and she slit open the pods and tossed the peas into her stew bowl.

"Hiya, everyone. Hey, Balder, how's that protective shield of oaths that Odin's ravens are gathering working out for you?" asked a familiar voice.

Loki! That tricky boygod was holding a bowl of stew and making a place for himself at the table by Yanis, on a stump across from Balder. What in the nine worlds was he doing here?

9
Food Fight

WITH A LOOK OF CONFUSION, THOR LEANED forward and cocked his head toward Loki, who now sat at the far end of the table from him. "I didn't know you were coming to Jotunheim."

Loki shrugged. "I wasn't. But school's out for the weekend, and my Yellow Fellows"—his nickname for his magic yellow shoes—"will fly me anywhere fast. So I figured why not come stay the night with you guys and hang around to cheer you on tomorrow?"

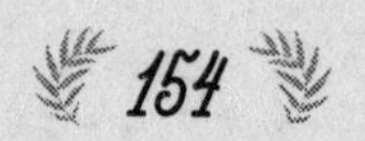

With that, Loki picked up a plum and tossed it up and down in the palm of one hand a couple of times. A mischievous grin came over his face as he glanced Balder's way once more. "So? Do you think Hugin and Munin have already secured an oath from a plum to never do you harm? Since they were getting promises from everything, I mean?"

"Why would Odin's ravens bother to get a promise from a plum? A plum couldn't harm anyone," remarked Ull, while helping himself to more bread and butter.

"I guess someone could choke on one, maybe?" suggested Honir after swallowing a spoonful of the bean stew.

Balder grinned. "The protection deadline is tomorrow morning—Saturday. So, I don't know if I'm protected from everything that could harm me yet or not, Loki. I didn't have any nightmares last night, which is a good sign. But go ahead and plum-bomb me if you want to test what happens." So saying, he pushed his stump stool back a bit from the table. Facing Loki, he offer himself as a target by spreading his arms wide.

Loki's face lit with impish glee. His dark-blue eyes darted sideways for an instant, toward the table of fire giants seated not far away. It was as if he was hoping they'd notice him. They hadn't, though. *And, anyway, why does he care?* Skade wondered.

Quickly Loki leaped up from his stool and stepped back from the table a few feet. Then he wound up his arm and let the plum he held fly. Toward Balder!

Thunk! As if there were an invisible stone wall surrounding Balder, the plum stopped about an inch from his nose. Then it abruptly it dropped into his lap. With a look of delight, he picked it up and popped it into his mouth. "Yum! Plum!"

Everyone at their table laughed.

Skade pumped a fist in the air. "Yes! Those ravens really did it! That protective shield Odin sought is working."

"It's like there's an invisible force field around you!" exclaimed Yanis, as she and Malfrid clapped in delight.

"I'm invincible!" said Balder. "Awesome. Food-bomb me some more," he begged the others. "This could be superfun!"

He didn't have to ask his friends twice. They began to pelt him with various veggies and chunks of bread. All bounced off him to hit the floor, and the students kept going.

Ull threw a hail of berries at Balder. This time, they boinged off and smacked the heads of some frost giants sitting nearby. *Oops!*

At the same moment, Loki launched a volley of hazelnuts at Balder. These bounced off to rain down on the fire giants' table. *Plop! Plop! Plop!* Soup sloshed out of bowls. Some of it splashed onto the flame-decorated sweater of one of the fire giants, who was *not* amused. He shoved back from the table, knocking over his stool. Then he turned a fierce and fiery glare on those at surrounding tables.

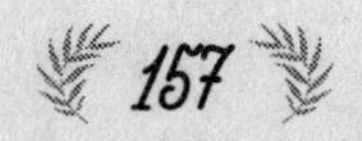

Skade eyed the wood stump on which he had been seated. It had been scorched by the heat he gave off! *Ymir's elbows!* The soup-splashed fire giant was none other than Surt! Or rather, Stupendously Scary Surt the Fire Giant, as she had mentally nicknamed him.

All the hotheaded (literally!) fire giants leaped to their booted feet and flew into battle mode, enlarging to five times Gruntery-acceptable size. Giant hands grabbed nuts, cheese chunks, fruits, and veggies from platters on feast tables. Arms drew back and fists clenched. They glared in every direction, unsure where to aim their ammo-food, but ready to pummel whoever was responsible. But then they all paused. Because the fire giants had no idea who had thrown the hazelnuts that had fallen into Surt's soup!

Any kind of battle was serious business, Skade knew. If something wasn't done to cut the tension and calm things down, this could definitely spin out of control! She jumped up to stand. Forcing a grin, she called out,

"Sorry about you getting splashed, Surt. It was an accident, promise." When he only glared at her, she hurriedly went on.

"Most of you probably don't know this," she shouted to the room at large, "but tossing food during dinner is considered sort of a sport where I go to school at Asgard Academy. It's called a food fight. And it's just for fun. Right, Freya?" Turning toward Freya, Skade shot her a look and then tossed a few berries across the table at her.

Quickly catching on to what Skade was trying to do, Freya tossed some pea pods back at her. Both girls giggled.

"See?" said Skade, turning back to the giants with her hands outspread. "Food fight. Get it? It's a *pretend* battle, and it's fun. Try it!"

Surt frowned. Then, very slowly, he picked up a hazelnut. And tossed it at Skrymir! Who then tossed a plum back. A few seconds passed. Then each tossed back another bit of fruit. And more, and more still.

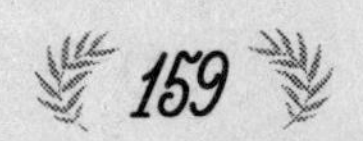

Other giants and students from the various worlds began to imitate them. Peas landed in Surt's hair and instantly went up in flames. *Zzzt!* Berries landed in Skrymir's hair and froze on impact. Soon many students were grinning and lobbing food. Before long, almost everyone in the Gruntery had joined in the fun. Wild plums, strawberries, auk eggs, and carrots were arcing high overhead to whack students way on the far side of the room. *Thwack! Splat!*

As Skade lobbed a handful of carrot slices toward another table, she couldn't help laughing merrily. A food fight probably wasn't what Odin had had in mind as a way to help all the worlds learn to get along. But, hey, whatever worked, right? Not only was the Gruntery filled with laughter now, but students from different schools had also begun to mingle. Giants were bumping congratulatory fists with dwarfs. Humans offered compliments on giants' good throws and vice versa.

After a while, some students started taking off for

the two igloos, still chatting and grinning and brushing away crumbs and splats of food from their clothing. "Ready to go?" Skade called to her friends.

"I am!" Yanis said.

"Me too," said Freya.

"Me three," added Malfrid.

"Let's make a run for it!" yelled Thor.

The whole AA team bolted for the Gruntery door, giggling and dodging flying food. Luckily they weren't leaving behind much messy cleanup for later because the dogs were happily scampering here and there to wolf down any ammo-food that hit the floor. However, as Skade raced from the table, she slid on a smooshed plum they'd missed. Her friends continued onward, not noticing. As she felt herself begin to slip, her arms spun.

A hand reached out to her. She grabbed onto it before she could hit the floor, then looked up to see . . . Njord? *He'd* helped her? "Uh . . . thanks," she said in surprise,

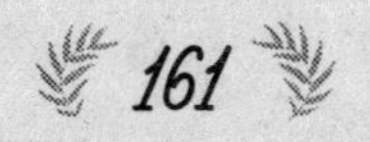

letting go of his hand as soon as she regained her balance.

"No problem," Njord replied, tucking his hands into his pockets. He looked around the room, then back at her. They were standing near the stage at one end of the room out of the line of food-fight fire. And as more students were leaving the Gruntery, less food was flying anyway.

"Well—" Skade began, making a move to go.

"That was smart thinking, what you said to the giants about food fights," Njord blurted out. "You probably saved us all from disaster."

Huh? Now Njord was complimenting her? Weird. She stared at him, half wondering if someone had put a magical niceness spell on him.

"So, um, have you decided who your aerial ski tricks partner's going to be in tomorrow's competition?" he asked before she could head off.

Skade stiffened. Aha! So Njord was only being nice

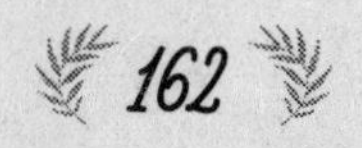

to her right now because he was hoping she'd choose him to be her partner? "No," she snapped.

He nodded, looking as if he wanted to say more. And for just a second, something in his earnest eyes made her wonder if maybe Njord felt a happy-melty feeling toward her. When her eyes rounded in surprise, all he did was mutter, "Yeah, okay. See ya," before moving out the door.

From somewhere nearby, she heard Yanis, Malfrid, and Freya chatting. They must have noticed she wasn't with them and had come back to find her. Freya was staring at the cafeteria's curtained stage. "I was talking to a frost giant earlier," she said to Skade as the girls came together. "He told me that tomorrow morning all the boys who want to be considered as a partner for the aerial ski tricks competition will be invited to line up on this stage behind the curtain."

"*Behind* the curtain?" Skade repeated, puzzled.

Freya nodded. "Yeah, and then you and those other

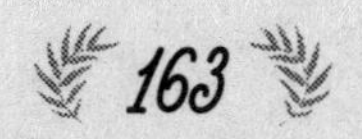

two girls that finaled in the competition will blindly choose a partner by pointing to their boots."

Malfrid cocked her head. "That's a weird way to do things. Unless the girls know a boy by his boots, they might not choose who they really want as a partner."

"Yeah, you could accidentally wind up with a poor skier," Freya said.

Skade flinched. This was exactly what she'd been thinking. Studying her, Yanis asked, "Who would you choose if you could pick any boy?"

"Hmm, let me think," said Skade tapping two fingers on her chin. Honir was a great cross-country skier, but he wasn't skilled at jumps. Ull and Thor had great power at downhill skiing, but as far as she knew, they weren't interested in performing acrobatic stunts. She didn't want to end up with that annoying Skrymir, either, or even worse—Surt! She didn't know anything about the skiers from other worlds—not really.

She certainly didn't want to partner with any of the

boys who'd laughed at her dancing in history class, so that ruled Njord out. Besides, she was almost positive he'd only complimented her on calming the giants to butter her up so she'd choose him as her partner. Which wasn't nice at all!

Hold up . . . *Balder!* He was *genuinely* nice. He'd tried to stop others from making fun of her dancing yesterday. Plus, he was a good all-around skier who was outstanding at trick jumps. Such kindness and skill should be rewarded.

"I'd choose Balder," she told her waiting friends.

A grin curved Freya's lips. "Somebody's crushing," she singsonged.

"What?! No, I'm not," sputtered Skade. She shook her head back and forth so hard that the black-and-white braid at her back flopped this way and that. "At least I don't think so. No, definitely not."

Then she recalled that happy-melty feeling she'd gotten when Balder was kind to her in Norse History.

Did she have a bit of a crush on that boygod? How was she supposed to know?

As she and her three friends moved toward the exit again, Skade's thoughts flew back to the competition. If she wanted to choose Balder, how could she make that happen? Glancing back at the stage, she studied its curtain. It hung as wide as the wooden stage itself. However, there was a six-inch gap of space between its bottom hem and the stage floor. Which meant she'd easily be able to see each of the boys' boots tomorrow when they stood onstage behind the curtain.

Every boy on her team had claimed to own only a single pair of boots apiece. She closed her eyes, trying to remember what Balder's looked like. She let out a frustrated huff because she had *no clue*! But she did know how to find out. Just ahead, her friends pushed the cafeteria door open.

"You coming to our igloo?" Freya called, pausing to look back at her.

Making up her mind, Skade waved her, Malfrid, and Yanis away with a smile. "Go on without me. I'll catch up in a few." Seconds later, she was also out the door, but scurrying in the opposite direction her friends had gone—toward the boys' igloo instead. If she was fast, she might catch sight of Balder's boots before he went inside for the night.

Jogging down the path, she came upon Loki. He was standing at the side of it, studying a vine that clung to the trunk of an aspen tree. She tiptoed past, relieved when he didn't notice her and ask why she was heading *away* from the girls' igloo. Besides not wanting to explain what she was up to, she was in a hurry!

Unfortunately, by the time she reached the boys' igloo, there were no boys in sight. Except for Loki, they must all be inside. Hoping against hope, she opened the outer door and stuck her head inside the boys' mudroom. Maybe she wasn't too late to catch a glimpse of Balder removing his boots.

Creeeek. Smells of leather and damp wool greeted her. But to her disappointment the mudroom was empty of boys, including Balder. Across the mudroom was a second door. It had been open to the common room earlier that day when Skade had brought the boys' stuff over from Freya's kittycart, so she knew that the boys' and girls' igloos were practically identical. Inside, there would be nine smaller zones along the circular wall where each team would sleep. Since those zones weren't all that big, when students weren't resting or sleeping, they'd probably be mingling out in the main space. It seemed that the igloos had been cleverly designed to get everyone to hang out and make friends!

Stepping inside the mudroom, Skade let the door swing shut behind her. The bags that she'd dropped off here earlier today were gone now, probably moved into the common room. Quickly, she studied the boots lined up on the racks set against the wall. There must be forty or fifty pairs of them, which made sense since there were close to a hundred students here at the games and about half of them were boys. Faced with so many boots, how would she ever figure out which pair belonged to Balder?

Creeeek. Suddenly the mudroom door she'd entered through opened behind her. A blast of cold air from outside hit her as a suspicious voice demanded, "What are you doing in here?"

Skade jumped around to see Loki. "Who, me? Nothing," she blurted quickly.

Only now she remembered that Loki had invited himself to stay overnight with the AA boys on the team. His distrustful gaze studied her, then fell on the boot racks. He was holding something small and green. A leafy twig. However, when he saw her glance toward it, he folded it in his palm, so she couldn't see exactly what kind of twig it was.

She glared at him and crossed her arms. "I'm not here to steal anything if that's what you're thinking," she huffed. "As if. Who wants stinky old boy boots? Not me."

Ignoring her, Loki's eyes stayed on the rack of boots. Now she began to wonder if he was looking for something there too. But what? Appearing a little disgruntled at not finding whatever he sought, he sat on a bench and began removing his yellow shoes.

Abruptly, the door that led into the main room opened and Balder stepped out into the mudroom too. He was barefoot . . . and holding a pair of boots! Brown ones, each with a white faux-fur cuff at the top and white leather straps that crisscrossed at the ankle.

"Oh! Hey, Skade, what are you, uh . . . um . . . ," Balder began. His words petered out when he noticed Loki was there too. "Well," he said to them both, "I forgot to take off my boots before I went inside, so . . ."

"Yeah, I do that all the time by accident," Skade told him truthfully. "Drives my podmates crazy when they trip over them in our room."

Grinning at her now, Balder went up to one of the racks and plunked his boots down in an empty space.

"Well, carry on, you guys. See you," he said, going back inside without being nosy about why they were there.

The minute he left, Loki jumped to his feet and went over to the rack. He set his shoes down right next to Balder's boots. With his back to Skade for a few seconds, he appeared to fiddle with one of Balder's boots. Huh? In her opinion, he was the one acting suspicious, not her!

"What are you doing?" She stepped to his side, staring at his and Balder's footwear on the rack.

"Just stowing my shoes. Why do you care?" asked Loki. Though his expression was calm, he sounded a little nervous at her question.

Skade shrugged. "I don't. See you tomorrow, Loki." After heading outside, she dashed down the path toward the girls' igloo. Now that she knew what Balder's boots looked like, she'd easily recognize them tomorrow. It would be a snap to choose him as her partner from the lineup behind the stage curtain.

Yay! Success! Pausing for a moment in the middle

of the path, she gave a happy skip and a twirl, just like Yanis might have done. As she did so, her eyes fell on the aspen tree where she'd seen Loki earlier. The vine growing on it was covered with green twigs. Now that she saw the twigs clearly, she recognized what they were. Mistletoe.

10
Enchanted Snow

THE NEXT MORNING BREAKFAST WAS delivered directly to the girls' igloo, while the boys went over to the Gruntery to eat and set up for the boot-choosing ceremony. Skade was wearing Freya's spiffy brown-and-gold tunic paired with her own olive green leggings and favorite boots. Feeling especially fancy, she was in a great mood as, after eating, she made her way to the cafeteria with the other girls.

The minute they arrived at the Gruntery, she went

to stand before the stage with Katrina and Olga, the other two ski jump finalists from yesterday's contest. Students from the various teams gathered to sit on the stump stools that had been placed in rows nearby, waiting to find out the girls' partner choices for the aerial ski tricks competition. About twenty-five boys—those hoping to compete—had lined up onstage behind the curtain.

Skade had scored the highest in yesterday's tryouts, so she got to go first. Briskly, she walked along the front of the raised stage, studying all the boots. When she passed a pair of red ones with orange and yellow flames painted up the sides, she gulped and walked faster. Surt? No way would she choose him. Or *any* of the scary fire giants!

When she came to a pair of brown boots with white leather straps crisscrossing at the ankles, she stopped and pointed. "I choose these boots," she announced.

Katrina and Olga made their selections as well.

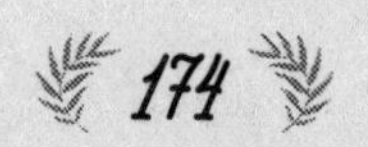

Then everyone in the Gruntery watched as the stage curtain was tugged higher to reveal the chosen boys' identities.

Smiling, Skade looked up into the face of the boy she'd picked. She gasped. Because the boy she'd chosen was not Balder. It was Njord! "You! Why are you wearing Balder's boots?" she demanded in confusion.

"Balder's out of the competition," Njord informed her as he hopped down from the stage. "He's got a bad case of mistle*toe*."

Her brows rose. "Meaning?"

"Meaning that a piece of that green stuff pricked his actual big toe." Njord shrugged. "Turns out he's allergic."

"Yeah," Honir chimed in as he also climbed down off the stage. "You should see his toe. It's swollen to almost twice normal size." Though the long-legged boygod hadn't been chosen by any of the girls, he remained his usual cheerful self. Thor and Ull hadn't been onstage at all, probably deciding ski tricks weren't their best sport. They and the rest of the AA team *had* been watching from nearby stump stools, however.

"Balder said he'll be okay hanging out in our igloo till we're all ready to leave after the competition ends," Thor told Skade now.

Freya frowned. "Poor Balder." She, Angerboda, Malfrid, and Yanis had come over and been listening in on Skade's conversation with the boys.

"I don't get it," Yanis said. "What about the oaths Hugin and Munin collected to make sure nothing could harm Balder? Why didn't those protect him?"

"Yeah," said Angerboda. "The ravens were supposed to have finished that task by now."

Along with the other teams, the Asgard group began moving for the exit door. "Hey, wait for me!" Loki called to them before anyone could answer Yanis. As they all turned toward him, he hopped off the edge of the stage and went to join them.

That Loki—always up to his sly tricks, thought Skade. Apparently he'd snuck onstage behind the curtain earlier, trying to get selected for the ski tricks competition even though he wasn't eligible since he wasn't *on* a team!

"I guess the ravens didn't suspect that mistletoe could harm anyone," Njord said as they all exited the Gruntery. "Odin sent an acorn message this morning telling Balder it was the only thing in the nine worlds they didn't bother to ask to swear an oath."

Once outside, they all grabbed their skis, which they'd placed in the ski racks next to the Gruntery earlier. "But I still don't understand why you're wearing Balder's boots," Skade said to Njord.

Not questioning how she knew they were Balder's boots, he only shrugged and said, "You know how nice Balder is. He offered to let me borrow them since there was no way he could ski in the competition after his toe

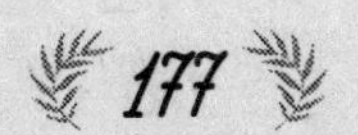

swelled up. My boots were pinching, remember?"

Skade nodded, and then her thoughts veered in another direction for a few seconds. Balder *was* nice. To everybody, not just her. Which meant *he* was treating her like everyone else and probably didn't feel any special happy-melty feelings toward *her*, she realized. *Hmm.* That realization didn't upset her actually. Which must mean she didn't have a crush on him, not really! *Phew!* What a relief.

In the distance, bright colors suddenly caught her eye. Three red flags, each with a blue cross outlined in white, stood atop a large snowbank. They'd been posted at the entrance to the ski slopes where the competitions would take place. It made her sad that she wouldn't compete in all three events, but at least she had one to look forward to. And she could cheer on the Asgard team during the others.

When all the teams moved toward the flags, she and Njord somehow wound up walking side by side, ahead of everyone else. It got quiet as they all huffed and puffed their way up the trail.

"I'm sorry, okay?" Njord said after the silence between them went on for a long time.

Surprised, Skade quirked an eyebrow at him. "Sorry for what?" There were just so many things he could be apologizing for in her opinion!

Njord sighed. "For what I said in history class Thursday. Your dancing wasn't all *that* bad."

"Wow, thanks, what a nice compliment," said Skade, rolling her eyes. She didn't want thoughts of that disaster to mess up her day, so she hoped he wouldn't say more. But he did.

"It's just that—" Njord began in an unusually serious tone. Interrupting himself, he started over. "I'm really sorry Balder's out of the games, but I'm glad you're in. Glad we'll be skiing together in the aerial event, and I—"

"What are you talking about? Wait, do you mean I'm

filling Balder's spot in all the competitions?" she asked.

By then, the rest of their team and Loki had caught up to them, and Ull overheard. "Yeah. Forgot to tell you," their team's captain informed her, "since Balder has officially dropped out of the competition, you'll be taking his place."

"Really?" she said in happy surprise as they all continued uphill. She *was* alternate, of course. And in an emergency, when a team member was unable to participate for whatever reason, an alternate could substitute.

"Or *I* could take his place," Loki offered quickly. He was walking alongside Angerboda. Since that girl liked him, like a *lot*, she'd looked happy to have his attention. However, now her face fell at the news that Skade would get to compete in all three events.

"Yeah, how about Loki instead?" Angerboda pushed, looking at Ull.

Njord eyed Loki. "No way. It's Skade's right to sub for Balder."

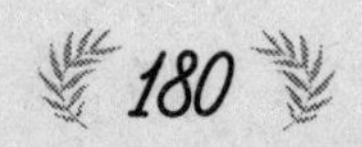

"True," said Ull. "Because as alternate she's already on the team." Then he added, "Poor Balder, though. It's a mystery how that mistletoe got into his boot."

"His boot?" echoed Skade. "The mistletoe that pricked him was in his boot?" Suddenly a puzzle piece fell into place. She stared at Loki, recalling how he'd seemed to fiddle with Balder's boots in the boys' mud-room last night. "Excuse us a minute," she told the others. "Loki and I need to talk."

"What about?" A look of alarm flashed over the boygod's face as she pulled him away from the group.

"You know what I think?" she hissed at Loki, while their companions went on ahead. "I think you booby-trapped Balder's boot with a spear of mistletoe last night. Somehow you knew he'd be allergic to it and were hoping to take his spot on the team." She stepped closer as a new thought came to her. "Maybe you even told the ravens mistletoe was harmless, even though you know Balder's allergic."

His eyes turned shifty. "How would I know that?"

"Because Balder told you at some point?" Skade bluffed. The shifty look on Loki's face told her she'd guessed right, but still he wouldn't admit his guilt.

"Wrong," he insisted. "Why would I want to be in this competition that badly?"

She thought a minute, but before she could go on, Njord appeared. Unnoticed by them, he'd remained behind to listen in. "Because you're hoping to impress Surt on the slopes," he accused Loki, jabbing a finger at his chest. "We guys have noticed how much you admire him and his sword. And everyone knows how easily you'll switch sides, backing gods or giants or whoever, depending on how it benefits or amuses you."

"You two don't know what you're talking about," scoffed Loki.

Skade raised an eyebrow. "Yeah, I think we do. So—"

Just then, a horn sounded. The games were about to kick off!

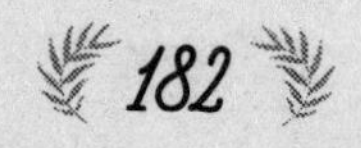

"Don't think this discussion is over," Njord told Loki as he and Skade turned to go.

"Yeah," Skade called back to Loki as she and Njord scurried to catch up with the other skiers at the top of the incline. "What you did to Balder was a real dirty trick, and you won't get away with it. We'll deal with you later!"

Loki just shrugged. He didn't even have the good grace to appear the slightest bit worried at their threats.

Three student competitors from the frost giant team now stood under the colorful flags at the entrance to the slopes. The flags whipped in the brisk winter wind. Skade shaded her eyes against the sunny blue sky overhead and studied the giants. She knew them all from her summers spent here in Jotunheim.

The girlgiant in the middle, who held a magic wand tucked in her belt, she recognized as Grid. To Grid's left was a girlgiant named Hyndla. She wore a silver-gray

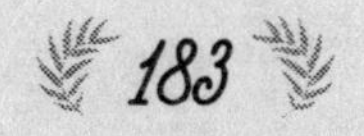

hangerock and a locket Skade knew contained a drawing of one of her pet greyhounds. The boygiant Skrymir stood to the right of Grid.

At their feet sat the gossipy Ratatosk, alongside a large, pretty red cage filled with straw. What was that for? Skade wondered. Did the squirrel sleep in it or something? She'd always assumed he slept somewhere within Yggdrasil's humongous branches.

"Welcome to Jotunheim's first ever ski games!" Grid called out to the nine teams once they'd all assembled under the flags. At this, everyone cheered. "Today's first competition will be an obstacle course down a ski run named Chilly Willy."

"Second will be relay race down a run called Yikes," Hyndla announced.

"And third will be the aerial ski tricks competition on the Cowabunga run," said Skrymir.

Skade heard Freya and Yanis giggle. Although she was used to them, those names *were* kind of funny.

"A panel of judges, one selected from each world, will determine the winners," Skrymir went on.

"Also, giants, listen up. To keep things fair, there'll be no enlarging today," added Hyndla.

There were a few grumbles over this from the two giant teams, but Skade hardly noticed. Getting more excited by the minute, she tugged her mittens snug. They were a bit misshapen. Of course they were, she mused fondly. Because Ms. Frigg had knitted them for her (and knitted mittens for many students at AA too).

Thinking of Ms. Frigg, Skade's gaze fell on Ratatosk. Over each of his shoulders, he carried two big bags of message acorns. He'd already pulled some out and was murmuring the names of the three ski runs chosen for the competitions to them before rolling each one off in a different direction. He would send out many more to various worlds this day to spread news of the competitions and their results as they occurred.

The gloves and acorns combined to nudge Skade's

conscience. There was something she needed to do, even if she *really* didn't want to. With a reluctant sigh, she reached into the pocket of her *hangerock* and pulled out the antler beanie Ms. Frigg had given her. She plopped it on her head, then tied its two braided brown yarn strings under her chin to secure it.

And then she waited for someone to laugh.

11
Snow Beasts

"HA-HA! WHAT IN THE NINE WORLDS IS that?" Loki asked, chuckling and pointing at her beanie. He'd had the nerve to follow her and Njord up the slope. "Talk about ri*donk*ulous. You should be embarrassed."

"Yeah, why did you put *that* on?" Honir said, shooting her a look of confusion. "Soon as other teams notice, they're going to make fun of us."

But Freya instantly guessed why she'd done it. "Skade's right," she told the rest of the Asgard team.

"Yeah. Put your beanies on, everybody. Ratatosk is here," added Yanis.

Malfrid nodded. "Mm-hmm. His acorns will report everything he sees. Or doesn't see, as in, *on top of our heads*." With that, those three girls whipped out their beanies and put them on.

"No! Not the antler beanies," begged Thor, backing away in horror.

Skade folded her arms and nodded. "Yup."

"They're right. We have to wear them," Ull agreed, but with a lack of enthusiasm in his voice. "Ms. Frigg will find out if we don't."

"And that would hurt her feelings." Njord sighed and pulled his beanie from his pocket.

"Oh, all right," said Angerboda, watching him put his on. Shoulders slumping, she and the rest of the AA team put on theirs, too.

"Gosh, too bad I don't have one," said Loki, not really looking at all sorry about that.

Taking his words at face value, Yanis suggested, "You could go borrow Balder's."

Loki's eyes slid over to where the fire giants' team stood a dozen feet away. Noting that Surt was already smirking at the beanies, Loki abruptly straightened and arranged his face into what Skade imagined he considered his "cool" expression.

"No, that's okay," Loki replied. "Balder might need his to keep his head warm while waiting around in that igloo."

Skade didn't buy Loki's seeming show of concern for even half a second. Obviously, he wasn't about to risk looking silly in front of his current fiery idol, even out of respect for Ms. Frigg's feelings!

As the Asgard team made their way to the top of Chilly Willy where the obstacle course event was about to begin, Skrymir noticed their new headgear. He began pointing and laughing. Not just a little bit. No, he fell on the snowy ground and rolled around, holding his sides

like they hurt from so much hilarity. Soon many other skiers were staring and giggling at them.

It took all the confidence Skade could muster to stand tall and call out to Skrymir, "What? Don't pretend. We all know you're just jealous of our awesome *lucky* antler beanies. Ms. Frigg made them for us, and we *love* them!"

Marching off with heads held high and proud, the whole Asgard team followed her up the mountainside. However, their cheeks were red, and not just from the cold air. Because having antlers sticking up from your head was embarrassing! Still, when Skade saw Ratatosk watching what was going on and sending out more message acorns, she knew her team was doing the right thing. Besides, she liked that her beanie was turning out to be cozy and warm!

"The views from up here are amazing," Yanis enthused once they reached the starting line atop Chilly Willy. Skade and the others all nodded in agreement,

gazing down at the glistening snow and the wisps of fog slowly threading through the treetops below.

"Aside from the fog and the usual rocks and trees jutting out from the sides, I don't see very many obstacles," Freya noted, studying Chilly Willy.

"Maybe they're farther down the piste?" suggested Njord, using a term that referred to a ski run of compacted snow.

The Asgard team looked to Skade and Angerboda, who knew the Jotunheim slopes better than any of them.

"I've skied Chilly Willy plenty of times. It's a black run, so a lot harder than a green or blue," said Angerboda. "I don't recall it having more obstacles than the usual rocks and trees jutting out here and there, though."

"On the bright side, it's fairly wide, which gives us room to maneuver. But it's also icy and steep," noted Skade. "And it's got a lot more moguls than I remember." She gestured toward numerous small hills of

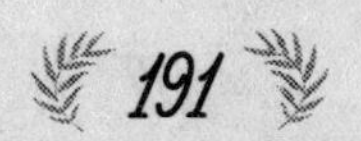

hard-packed snow. They'd been formed by skis making turns over and over in the same places.

Moments later, at the wave of a blue flag, all nine teams took off downhill at once. Skade zigzagged skillfully, avoiding any rocks, shrubs, and moguls in her path. That curling fog was pretty, but it also made it tough to see more than a few feet beyond her nose at times. However, soon she was leading the pack. So far, this event seemed easy-peasy!

Then, out of nowhere, she heard a *grrrowl.* She let out a little shriek. Because an enormous furry white figure with a scary grin on its face had leaped from beneath one of the moguls in the snow just ahead, its arms outspread as if to grab her. A polar bear? Standing up on its hind legs, it appeared to be twenty feet tall! Somehow she managed to shift her weight in time to turn her skis and dodge it.

"Ha! You missed me, Frosty!" she called back to it. But it had disappeared. Back into the mogul, she guessed.

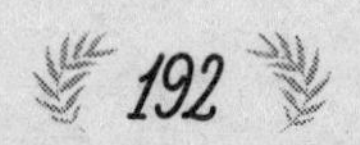

However, just a few yards on, a new figure sprang up from another mogul to make a grab for her. This time it was a gigantic white penguin! Pushing off hard with the pole in her right hand, she veered away in the nick of time. More such beasts began springing up from other moguls, one after another. They tried to block her and other skiers. These must be the obstacles. Obviously, they were made out of some kind of magical snow. Well, she would not let them defeat her!

Way over to her left, she saw Thor zooming downhill without poles, wearing a pair of iron gloves Sif had once given him as a gift. When a super-tall snow-walrus appeared a dozen feet in front of him, he tossed Mjollnir at it. However, he couldn't throw that hammer fast enough to save himself. Too off balance to successfully veer around the beast, he took a tumble and wound up sprawled in a snowbank. Immediately he stuck one arm straight up in the air and handily caught his hammer as it returned to him. (Which it always did.)

Coming up from behind Skade fast now, Skrymir whizzed by on his skis, easily avoiding the snow-lynx that leaped into his path. From all sides of her, Skade heard shrieks as additional snow creatures popped up from moguls here and there to send students tumbling in every direction. Yet the frost giants were having no problem, she realized. They somehow managed to zoom around every beast that sprang up.

No, wait. They weren't zooming *around* them. They were zooming *through* them! And afterward, the beasts disappeared until another skier came along. This could only mean that the beasts were made of enchanted snow!

Skade watched as Skrymir ran right through the middle of a large snow-squirrel. *Poof!* It simply disappeared. Of course! That sneaky Skrymir was skilled in magic, able to create illusions to make you to see things that didn't really exist. Like fake snow beasts.

Cheaters! The frost giants knew they weren't real, so

they didn't even try to avoid them. No fair for them to be the only ones with this information. By the time the rest of the teams figured out what was going on, they'd be too far behind to ever catch up. Skrymir was trying to ensure that his team would win this event. He was just as bad as Loki with his magic tricks. Maybe worse!

As Skade zoomed haphazardly down the slope, yet another enchanted beast suddenly sprang out only two feet in front of her. A giant snow-moose! Even knowing it was fake, she instinctively dodged it. This caused the tips of her skis to hit a mogul straight on. Whoa! As she went flying into the air, she curled into a tight ball, expecting the worst as she came tumbling back down.

Crack! She slammed onto the icy, packed snow, smacking the back of her head. She waited for a headache to start pounding. For pain to come. But it didn't.

"You okay?" It was Njord. He'd skied over to help her.

Sitting up, Skade raised a hand to her head. The soft, knitted antler beanie she wore was no longer soft.

She took it off. Staring at it, she knocked her knuckles against the invisible layer of hardness that now covered it. "I'm fine. Not hurt at all," she told Njord. "I think Ms. Frigg's antler beanies have some kind of magical safety feature in them. Mine saved me when I fell and hit the ice."

Njord relaxed, looking relieved. "She did mention that the beanies were protective gear."

"Yeah, but until now, I didn't fully appreciate what that meant," said Skade. "They're like safety helmets or brain armor." She grinned at him.

"Good thing, too," said Njord, grinning back.

"Right, I'd be toast if I hadn't been wearing this," said Skade, plopping her beanie back on her head and tying its strings under her chin. "Bruised and broken toast."

Njord's smile widened. Hand out to her, he tugged her up. "If the rest of the events are this dangerous, our team is going to need all the protection we can get."

"True," she replied dusting crusty snow from her clothes. Eating her friend Idun's magical apples of youth kept the goddesses and gods forever young, but the apples did *not* make them immortal. They could die if injured badly enough.

"C'mon, let's get going," said Njord. But before they could continue downhill, a great quaking began. It felt as if they were trapped inside a huge snow globe being shaken by a giant unseen hand. Next, they heard a roaring sound and whirled around to look uphill.

"What now?" Njord said worriedly. Turned out, he was right to be anxious. Because behind them, a roaring avalanche was now hurtling their way! Not a snow avalanche, however. An avalanche of *water*.

Skade gasped. In the distance, Surt stood on a tall peak. He'd drawn his infamous flaming sword and was approaching a snow beast! With each swish he wielded, the sword shot flames in every direction, liquifying everything in their path.

"The fire giants! Surt's trying to *melt* the enchanted snow beasts," she exclaimed. "But they're not actually real, just an illusion, and his fire sword is turning *everything* that's frozen to water."

Njord frowned. "Not to mention burning down all the trees alongside the run!"

Suddenly a big wave of frosty water rushed downhill and slammed into the fire giants. To Skade's surprise, Stupendously Scary Surt shrieked like a baby as he and his drippy pals were carried along by the whooshing water. She saw Loki hovering in his yellow shoes over a large rock nearby, watching the spectacle. He looked shocked, obviously disappointed in his idol's wimpy behavior.

"Oh no!" Skade wailed to Njord as the water whooshed their way. "Too bad we don't have Frey's ship."

"*Skidbladnir?* Wait—I do! Frey loaned it to me to sail while he's away." Quickly, he pulled Frey's magic

expandable ship from his pocket. They both pulled off their skis, then tossed them and themselves into the ship as it enlarged around them. The magical ship automatically hoisted its sail, causing a wind to fill it and blow them safely along the top of the moving water. As they sailed downhill, they rescued anyone they found on the way, and the ship magically expanded to accommodate them all.

Skrymir's trickery had put him way ahead. But as the rush of water got louder, Skade saw him glance to see what was going on behind him. Just then, another enchanted snow beast popped up in front of him. This one was shaped like a giant rabbit with tall ears and two long front teeth. Taken off guard by its sudden appearance when he turned again to face forward, Skrymir startled even though the creature wasn't real. Automatically veering, he ran into another frost giant, and they both took a tumble. *Splash!* The oncoming water swiftly overtook them.

Seeing Ull and Honir swept up in the water some distance away, Njord called out to them with advice on how to use their skis on water, by moving back and forth in wide zigzags. As the boygod of the sea, it was a skill he knew well! Soon those boys were safely water-skiing atop the rushing water. Watching them, others on the slopes caught on and began doing the same, skimming along the water avalanche as it hurtled them all downhill.

Skade grinned and waved at Skrymir as they passed him by. He was a great snow skier but wasn't doing so well at waterskiing. Instead, he had kicked off his skis and was slowly swimming his way downhill. At that rate, he'd probably finish last!

"Ha! A *rabbit* scared you into crashing? Cheaters never win!" she called to him, causing an embarrassed frown to cross his face.

Eventually the rushing water slowed to pool at a low spot near the finish line, forming a lake. Skade, Njord, and those they'd rescued jumped ship. As they spilled into the lake, they shivered. Because that water was freezing cold! Luckily, like with the Spring of Mimir, once they stepped out of the lake, all became magically dry again.

After it was empty, *Skidbladnir* had shrunk, and now Njord stowed it in his pocket. He and Skade glanced around and saw that all the teams were searching for their members. She waved to the rest of the AA team, which had wound up safely across the lake from them.

Before she could call out to them, however, a cute, tiny voice spoke up from somewhere near her feet. "Balder's gone!"

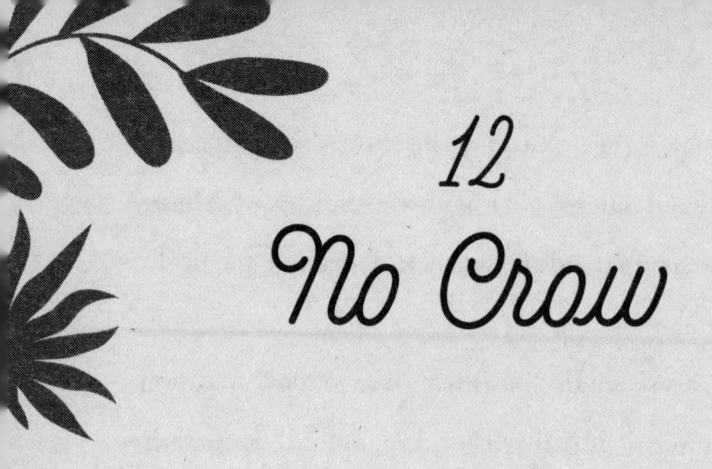

12
No Crow

STANDING LAKESIDE NEXT TO NJORD, SKADE glanced down to see a message acorn rolling around her booted feet. "Balder's gone? You mean to Asgard?" she asked it.

"No, not to *there*," singsonged the acorn.

"Where, then?" Skade asked, squatting down to better hear its reply.

"Balder's in Helheim," replied the acorn before rolling away.

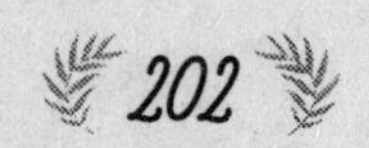

Skade gasped. She and Njord exchanged a horrified look. Spotting Ratatosk scampering past, Njord shouted out to him. "Is it true? Is Balder in Helheim?"

"Of course! Got it straight from the dragon's mouth," the squirrel informed them. "I was down in Niflheim just now, gathering gossip, er . . . I mean, *news* from Nidhogg. That dragon keeps a sharp eye on the third-ring worlds. He told me that Hel has stolen Balder away to Helheim."

Skade paled at this news. If there was one place Balder didn't belong, it was in Helheim! That world was home to the *evil* dead, and Hel was the female monster who basically babysat them and foiled any escape plans they hatched.

"What a big news day! Snow beasts, a water avalanche, Balder in Helheim!" said the squirrel, rubbing his paws together in delight. "I'm off to spread the scoop everywhere, all the way up to that nosy eagle at the top of Yggdrasil. Gotta go! Don't want Nidhogg

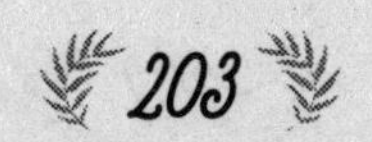

to beat me to it. For some reason, that dragon has decided to race me throughout the worlds to deliver the news!"

Ratatosk took off in a series of leaps across the snow, leaving paw prints behind him while he tossed out message acorns as if they were gossip-sprouting seeds. Which they kind of were.

"We've got to rescue Balder!" Njord exclaimed. "Who knows what that monster in Helheim and the evil ones she babysits plan to do with him?!"

For a split second, Skade thought how going after Balder could mean that Asgard would lose the upcoming relay race, disqualified for having too few members. And she'd miss her chance to triumph in the aerial ski tricks event too! But what was more important? Winning games? Or helping a friend in trouble? She didn't have to consider twice.

"Okay, I know a shortcut to Helheim from here," she told Njord. She pointed to a large forest some dis-

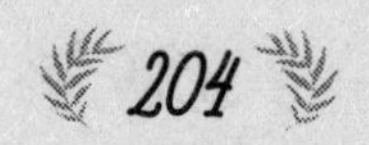

tance away. "It's through those trees, then down a ski slope called (*Gulp!*) Helrun."

Using hand gestures, pointing toward the forest and calling out across the lake, she tried to convey to their distant team the mission they were about to undertake. Yanis and Freya signaled back that they'd mostly understood and would tell the others.

As Skade skied into the forest with Njord, an involuntary shiver ran through her. She could hardly believe she'd suggested that they traverse the treacherous Helrun. Ever since she'd lost control and tumbled down it, the idea of going anywhere near it terrified her.

"Why do you think Hel took Balder?" Njord mused as the two of them pushed through the forest with skis and poles, gliding around trees and rocks. "Think she hopes his kindness will be a good influence on those evil dead she babysits?"

Privately, Skade was worried Hel had taken Balder for a very different reason. Had that mistletoe made

him sicker that they'd realized? Even turned him rotten somehow? Would he soon fit in with the evil dead?

"I guess we'll find out" was all she said. No reason to make Njord more worried too. An hour later, they were through the forest. Directly ahead of them was the Helrun. Skade shuddered, and not just from the cold.

A look of alarm came over Njord's face as he considered the perilously long, steep, narrow, icy chute. "One wrong move and we'll wind up skiing on our faces the whole way down it," he remarked.

"Yeah, been there, done that," Skade informed him. "C'mon, let's go. I don't want to overthink it. We'll just have to be very, *very* careful."

Cautiously, she positioned herself at the top of the run, ski tips forward. Her heart was beating fast. The sun behind them threw their bluish, antler-headed shadows across the snow. The shadowy sight made her giggle and relax a bit. Ms. Frigg's beanie had protected her when she fell. Maybe the beanies would protect them both

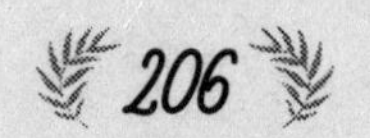

now and even bring them the luck they would sorely need to save Balder from Helheim! That thought lifted her spirits.

Odin's words came back to her: *Every time I faced down a fear, no matter how big or small, I gained courage and strength.* She could do this! She pushed off. *Whoosh!* Down, down, down she shot through the narrow chute, with Njord close behind her.

In seconds they were whizzing down the Jotunheim mountains, across the second ring, and beside one of Yggdrasil's three roots past a spring called Hvergelmir. Eventually the Helrun sent them across a golden bridge and zoomed them along the banks of the raging Gjoll River.

This river was boiling hot and full of warriors who hurled magical bubbles at whoever passed by. Whenever the bubbles hit Skade, Njord, or the snowy ground nearby, they exploded into loud insults. "Those antlers are stupid!" "Losers! You think you're reindeer or something?" "Weirdos!" It was a like a game of dodgeball, only instead of dodging silent rubber balls, they dodged bubbles that were steaming hot, loud, and mean!

Finally Skade and Njord arrived at a gate guarded by a terrifyingly huge dog who snarled and barked ferociously upon seeing them. After swishing to a stop, they stood before the gate, breathing hard from their exertions, and eyed him.

Despite the trials that were surely still to come, a thrill filled Skade. She'd done it! She'd found the confidence within to conquer the horrible Helrun! She could hardly wait to tell Angerboda. If they ever managed to get back to Jotunheim, that was.

"This . . . must be . . . Helheim," Njord said between tired, huff-puff breaths. "It looks . . . like the carving of that world . . . on the door of our Norse History class. Phew! It's hot down here."

"Yeah, and stinky," added Skade, wrinkling her nose. Noticing a strange glow, she peered through the iron bars of the gate. She elbowed Njord and pointed. "There's Balder!"

Their friend sat some distance away upon a small throne. Relief filled her that he didn't appear sick or dead, as she had feared. This world was so dark and gloomy that the pale glow of his skin made him look sort of like a boy-shaped lamp. A lamp that was reading aloud to a crowd of hundreds of evil dead that sat around him, entranced by the story.

A large book made of thin sheets of tree bark lay open upon his lap. The boots on his feet were way too big for him, probably borrowed from some other Helheim dweller to fit his swollen mistle-toe. Too bad he wasn't wearing his antler beanie. It might've protected him from harm. Then she noticed that someone else was wearing it. Hel!

Beanie atop her long gray hair, she sat beside Balder on a huge throne built of animal bones (*yikes*), happily listening to Balder as she crocheted something. Both thrones were perched upon a single raised platform, behind which rose a high, dark, craggy rock wall. Every now and then she or one of the crowd around Balder would cackle, as if something he read aloud amused them.

"With all those evil characters in there, it'll be dangerous to enter," Skade murmured to Njord as they stood outside the iron-barred gate.

"And almost impossible to leave again, unless Hel allows it," he agreed. Mr. Sturluson had taught them that.

Skade straightened. She was no scaredy-rabbit, no matter what Skrymir liked to think. They'd come here to rescue Balder. They had to at least try! She pushed through the unlocked gate, but then paused mid-step when the guard dog strained at his leash, barking and snarling.

"Down, Garm! Good boy," Hel called to the dog. At this, he rolled over onto his back. His tongue hung out and his mouth spread into a silly (but evil-looking) grin.

Skade and Njord made their way closer to the

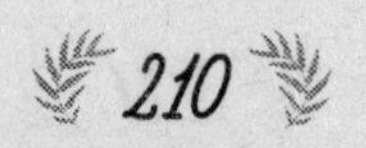

thrones, but Balder continued to read without looking up from his book. "Probably under an enchantment," Skade whispered to Njord.

Hel noticed them, though. She tossed aside her crochet project and glared down her long, pointed nose at them. "Who are you? What do you want?" she demanded.

"We are the girlgoddess Skade and boygod Njord, students from Odin's academy in Asgard," Skade announced.

"We've come for Balder," Njord added.

"Balder? Who's he?" Hel bluffed.

"You know who he is," said Skade, pointing. "He's sitting right next to you."

Hel grinned, displaying green teeth. "Ha! Got me! I had a feeling his dreamy, kind voice would have a calming effect on these hooligans I watch over here in Helheim. And I was right. Usually, they're running around making trouble. But see how calm they are?"

"Dreamy?" Skade echoed. A new thought struck her.

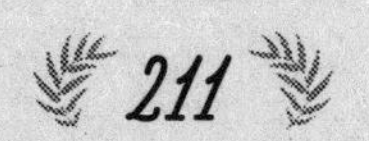

"Did you plant all those giant nightmares in Balder's head? The ones he got just before we came to Jotunheim for the ski competition?"

Hel shrugged. "I won't deny it. I used the confusion at Jotunheim to my advantage. I wove his dreams to make him sleepwalk here. And here he'll stay."

"So you brought Balder to Helheim to be their . . . stand-in babysitter?" asked Njord, pointing toward the evil dead. "That's so selfish!"

"Everyone in all the worlds likes Balder," said Skade. "You can't keep him down here where no one else can ever see him," she insisted.

"Oh, I can do exactly that. This is my world. I decide the fate of all those who enter my realm. Including you two," said Hel. Her eyes gleamed with power.

Fear shot through Skade.

"But poor Balder. He'll be so bored," Njord began.

Hel straightened, her face flushing with anger. "Are you saying my world and I are boring?"

"No, of course not," Skade said quickly. "We don't even know you or your realm, really. Tell us, please, what can we do to get you to release Balder to us, return his antler beanie, and give us all safe passage from this world? We'll do anything."

"Anything?" Hel's gray eyes sparkled in the gloom. "Very well. On the strength of your offer I will agree to release Balder and also both of you."

Skade clasped her palms together. "Oh! Thank you so much, we—"

Hel held up her hand to stop her from going on. "On one condition."

Uh-oh, thought Skade. She had a feeling that condition wouldn't be an easy one.

Hel sat forward on her throne, squinting at them through the gloom. "If Balder is as precious as you say, then he must be beloved by all things living and dead. And none would be happy about his poor swollen toe, right? So if you can get one thing living and one thing dead to cry for him in the next five minutes, I'll release him. However, if you can't, he must remain here in Helheim. And the two of you must stay as well. Forever. Deal?"

Skade and Njord looked at each other. They really had no choice but to agree. With a deep, worried sigh, both of them replied, "Deal."

Smiling, Hel sat back in her throne. "Your five minutes begin . . . *now*."

Skade and Njord bent close to talk in private. "How are we going to do this? I mean, getting a living thing to cry isn't that hard. *I* can cry," Skade whispered. "But how can we make something that's *dead* weep?"

"Go ahead and start your crying while I think on how to make somebody in that crowd of dead weep." Njord nodded toward the evil group listening to Balder read.

"Okay, I'll think sad thoughts. Here goes," said Skade.

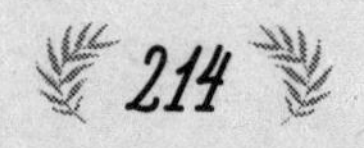

Closing her eyes, she thought of the day she'd gotten the invitation from Odin informing her that she was being summoned to a new school called Asgard Academy. She'd been very sad to leave her old friends and also worried about making new ones. In fact, she *might've* actually wept that day. (Not like a crybaby or anything, she decided quickly.) Unfortunately, this once-sad thought didn't bring tears now. Why? Because she had grown to love AA and the new friends she'd made there!

Now what? She tried imagining a giant snow beast gobbling all thirteen pairs of her boots, which she'd carefully picked out and purchased. Although that thought was unhappy, it occurred to her that getting to buy new replacement boots would be fun. Nope, no tears came over that, either. *Argh!*

She gazed around Helheim. It was gloomy and sad. None of her new podmate friends were here. She forced herself to think about the possibility that she, Njord, and Balder might be stuck here forever if they weren't able to meet Hel's condition for Balder's release. After a minute, nine tears rolled down each of her cheeks. Success!

Noting her tears, Hel remarked, "Whatever. So you made yourself—something living—cry. Big whoop. Now for the hard part. Make something not-living cry."

Skade brushed her tears away, smiling hopefully at Njord. His eyes were fixed on the group of evil dead. As she watched, he poked and prodded one after another of them, as if that might produce tears. But nothing happened. Maybe, being dead and all, they couldn't feel pain. Or maybe they were too enchanted by Balder's story to notice anything else. Whatever. Time was nearly up.

"Try making something else that's not alive cry instead of those evil dead guys," Skade suggested. "After all, you're boygod of the sea."

"So?" he said, sounding stressed.

"So . . . tears . . . seas . . . waterfalls, it's all the same stuff really," she whispered encouragingly. "Just salt water. You're good at bringing that forth."

"You're right," he said, seeming to relax. Looking beyond her, he fixed a determined gaze on the wall of rock beyond Hel's and Balder's thrones. He stared hard at the wall, as if willing something to happen. For a long moment, nothing changed. Then, ever so slowly, salt water began to seep out of the rock. More and more fell until it became a waterfall. Soon a small moat formed around the raised area upon which the two thrones were perched. Noticing it, the evil dead stopped attending to Balder's story. They jumped into the moat and began frolicking and swimming.

Grinning with glee, Skade and Njord high-fived each other. "We did it!"

To their surprise, Hel clapped her hands in delight. "You made me a waterfall! And a swimming pool, both with cool water? Perfect! It's so hot down here, that's

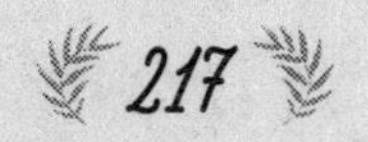

half the reason the evil dead are so unhappy. Now I can keep them in line by rewarding them with a swim if they behave."

Humph. *Would it hurt her to say thank you?* Skade thought. Hoping to teach Hel a bit of politeness, she prompted. "That was nice of Njord, don't you think? So what do you say?"

"I say, 'You win.' Goodbye. And I'm keeping the beanie," said Hel. Getting up from her throne, she grabbed Balder and tossed him over the moat to Skade and Njord. Fortunately they caught him and set him on his somewhat unsteady feet.

"Huh? Where am I?" he murmured as Hel waved them all away. Together, Skade and Njord explained what had happened as they helped Balder hobble back through Helheim's gate.

Once outside, they were surprised to see Freya's kittycart swooping in a circle overhead. "I heard Balder had been kidnapped, and my jewel Brising told me where to find you," she shouted down to them. Swiftly she landed nearby and waited for them.

After Skade, Njord, and Balder were safely in the cart, Freya called to her magical gray tabby cats. "Fly, kitty, kitty!" Her long, glittery pale-blond hair had come loose from her braids and fanned out behind her as she flew with them toward Jotunheim to grab their belongings before returning home to Asgard.

"The second and third competitions were canceled due to all the trouble during the first one," Freya informed them as they flew. "So everyone has begun to return to their own worlds."

"Oh, that's too bad," said Skade. "Odin had such high hopes for the games' potential to improve relations between the worlds. Failed hopes, I guess."

Freya flicked her a glance. "That's not all. The news gets worse. Maybe much worse. Some weirdly familiar things have begun happening, have you noticed? Things that could mean the beginning of Ragnarok."

Skade and the two boys gasped. The coming of Ragnarok would mean the end of Yggdrasil. All nine worlds would be destroyed. It was too horrible to imagine!

"Like for instance," Freya went on, "we know that Ragnarok will take place in winter."

"*Check.* It's already winter," said Balder, who seemed more or less back to normal now, except for his still-swollen toe.

One by one, they continued checking off the list of events that they'd all been taught would lead up to that terrible end of all the worlds.

"There will be a great fire. *Check.* Not only did that fire giant's sword melt the snow, but the forest on one side of the run also burned to the ground, remember?" said Njord.

Freya nodded. "Mighty Yggdrasil will shudder and quake. *Check.* We felt its limbs shudder when that water avalanche started."

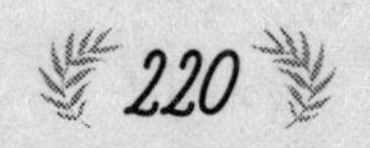

"A great serpent will be unleashed. *Check.* Ratatosk told me today that Nidhogg had suddenly decided to race him up to the top of Yggdrasil," announced Skade.

"There will be monsters. *Check.* The snow beasts could count as monsters," Njord said.

"Hel, down in Helheim, too," suggested Balder.

They were closing in on Jotunheim now. Up ahead, Skade could see the twin igloos and the red, blue, and white flags that marked the area of the ski games. "The only two things left to cause Ragnarok to begin are for the alarm in the Valhallateria to sound five hundred and forty blasts," she mused. "And then roosters would have to crow."

"Phew," said Balder. "I haven't heard any alarms *or* any crowing." His words were barely out of his mouth, however, when short, sharp blasts—too many and too fast to count—began to sound rapidly. "*Ymir's ears!* I spoke too soon," Balder wailed. Even though the Valhallateria was quite far away, its alarm had been specially designed to be heard in all nine worlds. "If roosters crow next, we are doomed!" moaned Balder.

Skade glanced at the horizon where the first fingers of sunset pink were curling. "Roosters normally crow in the mornings. So these would have to be roosters that crow at nightfall for some reason. Ragnarok could still be prevented if we can find and stop them in time."

"Oh no!" said Njord. When everyone turned his way, he pointed toward the ground below them under the flags. "See that red cage? The one near the starting line of Chilly Willy? Skrymir told me that the fire giants brought it as a gift that would somehow signal the end of the games today. And look!"

As they watched, all on its own, the cage door began to magically open. From overhead, they could see three roosters snuggled upon the straw within the cage. At the sound of the door creaking open, the roosters woke. They hopped out. Their beaks parted, and . . .

"They're going to crow!" yelped Balder.

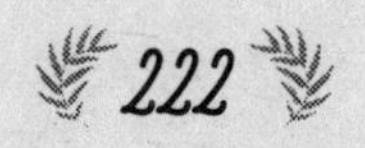

"We have to stop them!" cried Skade, shouting to be heard over the ongoing alarm.

"Whoa, kitty, kitty!" Freya called. Her two tabby cats banked against the wind to slow their flight. They landed below the tall flags. Claws out, the cats skidded to a halt right in front of the cage and the roosters.

"No crowing!" Skade, Freya, Njord, and Balder yelled, rushing toward them and wildly waving their arms.

Surprised, the roosters squawked. But they did *not* crow! Instead, in a flap of feathers, they did a series of hops and then flew off in different directions to roost in the branches of nearby fir trees.

Instantly the alarm went silent. Skade high-fived Freya. "Your cats helped us scare the crow out of those roosters. Their cock-a-doodle-doos stayed cock-a-doodle-don'ts. We saved the worlds!"

"Good job, *silfrkatter*," Freya said, using a term that meant "silver cats." She gave them pets and kisses.

Meow! Meow!

13
Confi-dance

BACK AT ASGARD ACADEMY, THE SCHOOL dance was about to begin. Freya's cart touched down just in time for Skade, Freya, Njord, and Balder to join their teammates in going. (The rest of their team had returned earlier via the system of slides that took them up to the Heartwood Library.) It had been a long day, and everyone was tired.

But when they entered the Valhallateria and were greeted with cheers, music, and snacks, their spirits lightened and they became eager for fun. Fellow students had pushed the tables and chairs against the walls and decorated for the event. Suspended by magic, hundreds of silver snowflakes sparkled and twirled beneath the ceiling. The sculpted warriors in the paintings that covered the walls even wore party hats. There was apple spice cake, apple juice, and lots more to snack on.

Ratatosk and his message acorns had done their work. Everyone at school already knew what had gone on in Jotunheim and Helheim. They gathered around to hug their beloved Balder, happy that he was okay.

Even though the games had been canceled, students seemed extra excited to celebrate the fact that the Asgard team had scored highest overall in the Chilly Willy obstacle course event, despite Skrymir's trickery. And that Skade had aced the tryouts for the aerial ski tricks competition, even if she and Njord had never gotten to perform together as partners. And, of course, everyone was grateful that Ragnarok had been avoided, at least for now.

Best of all was Odin and Ms. Frigg's pride in the team. They made an appearance in the Valhallateria soon after the AA team arrived and congratulated each member individually in front of the whole school.

"We're sorry all the worlds didn't get along as well at the games as you'd hoped," Skade told the coprincipals afterward.

"Small steps," said Odin, appearing more pleased than she'd expected. "Your team did your best in a difficult situation. You extended the hand of friendship to the other worlds. It could be the start of something good. I have a feeling there will be fun food fights in the cafeterias of at least some of those far-flung worlds in the future."

At this, they all laughed.

"I think the Jotunheim competition was a good plan, even though it didn't work out perfectly. Maybe we could try again sometime?" Angerboda put in, surprising everyone with her upbeat suggestion.

"Good idea," voices called out from the crowd.

"I'm thinking we should split the teams up differently next time, though," said Thor. "Mix things up a little."

"Great idea!" Skade seconded. "There could still be nine teams. But the members of each team would come from different worlds. That way, while skiing together, everyone on a team can learn more about one another's school and world."

The usually grumpy Angerboda looked pleased at their support and suggestions. For the first time, hope filled Skade that someday they might actually become more friendly. Maybe things could change for the better among the worlds. Maybe they already were.

Odin and Ms. Frigg looked at each other. Apparently thinking the same thing, they smiled big. Then they proclaimed the students' ideas to be "perfect!"

"But for now, there's food . . . and dancing," Odin announced in his powerful voice. He motioned toward the ceramic goat fountain and the snack-laden tables near it. With his other hand he gestured toward Bragi and Fossegrim, who were seated nearby. Bragi immediately began to strum his lute, and Fossegrim took up his fiddle.

"Everyone, enjoy!" Odin and Ms. Frigg finished together as the music began.

Dancing? *Uh-oh.* Skade looked toward the exit door. But before she could seriously consider sneaking out, her friends dragged her with them onto the dance floor. There weren't any boys out there—not yet, anyway—but lots of girls seemed to be having fun together. And suddenly Skade didn't *want* to miss out.

When she started to dance, however, she heard snickers. Whipping around, she saw that Loki was over on the sidelines mimicking the way she was dancing. That meanie. However, it was nice to note that no one else was making fun of her.

Frowning, Skade folded her arms. "If you think I'm so bad, let's see if you can do any better," she called out to him loudly. Freya, Sif, and Idun came to stand on either side of her. They also frowned at Loki.

"Uh . . . um . . ." Loki shuffled his magic-yellow-shoe-clad feet, looking embarrassed. "I don't see why I should have to be the first guy to dance," he whined. Looking at the other boys, he said, "One of you go first."

The boys all took a step back. Apparently they were willing to practice traditional dance steps in history class—because they *had* to—but when it came to the more self-styled dancing of a school dance, they were too chicken to try. Who was the scaredy-rabbit now?

"Do it," Skade told Loki. Then, remembering their unfinished discussion about what he'd done to Balder, she added, "Or I might have to tell Odin about your behavior at the games. Like your admiration of Surt, and the mistle—"

Loki cut her off, saying, "You can't prove anything.

And Surt's sword *is* cool, but he turned out to be a drippy wimp." Then, before anyone could say more, he zoomed away to the snack tables.

"Loki shouldn't have made fun of your dancing," Njord said after coming over to stand near Skade. "And you know, last Thursday in history class . . . I only said what I said to show off. To be cool in front of the guys. I'm sorry I acted mean."

Skade raised an eyebrow. "Okay."

Shifting nervously from one foot to the other, Njord asked, "Is there anything I can do to make things up to you?"

Skade considered this. They'd been through so much together the past few days that she thought maybe she really was ready to forgive him for his teasing. Then an idea came to her. Njord looked a little worried at the mischief that lit her eyes when she replied, "Yes." Then she said, "You can make me laugh. Do a dance so silly that my friends and I all crack up."

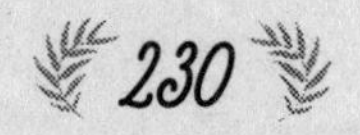

"Um . . . ," said Njord, looking nervous.

"C'mon. You owe me. Where's your confidence?" she said to him. Then she raised her gaze to take in the whole room—boys and girls alike. "We want to see *all* the boys do some silly, goofy, dorky dancing. Right, girls?"

The girls grinned, nodding. The boys, however, shuffled their feet and looked sheepishly at one another. Skade could practically see the emotions warring within Njord. Then he surprised her.

"All right, guys, let's show these girls we can make 'em laugh!" he declared, stepping up to the challenge. "Since I feel kind of chicken about doing this, I'll do a chicken dance. P-kawk!" With that, he bent his elbows like wings and jerked his chin back and forth while hopping around in time to the music. He was cluck-dancing! And it was hilarious. So hilarious it actually did make Skade laugh. Her friends, too. Seeing how much fun he was having and how much positive attention he was getting, the other boys joined in, copying him and adding funny hops and spins.

Even the teachers got into the act. Mr. Sturluson tossed his red hat high, then spun around in time to catch it before tossing it again. And the warriors in the wall paintings danced too! Skade kind of wished Odin hadn't left early. What kind of dance might he have done?

Suddenly Njord danced up beside her. "C'mon," he said. "Since we didn't get to partner for the aerial ski tricks event, here's our chance . . . to dance."

He didn't have to ask her twice. She began cluck-walking and wing-flapping alongside him. When they passed their history teacher, she grinned at him. "That hat dance you're doing is not at all traditional," she told him, smiling as she and Njord *p-kawk*ed by.

He smiled back. "You're right. But now that I think about it, all traditions were once nontraditional. New traditions are being made all the time. Like the chicken dance." She could hardly believe it when he started copying them!

Hearing a shriek of surprise minutes later, she turned to see one of Thor's pet goats butt Loki's rear end. This caused him to spill apple juice on his favorite yellow shoes, which the goat began to nibble.

Loki backed away. "Shoo! Shoo!"

"Yeah! That's right, go for that tasty *shoe*!" Thor called out to his goat, laughing.

Apparently deciding the yellow shoes were indeed tasty, the goat began chasing Loki all over the Valhallateria. Finally, desperate to keep the goat's teeth away from his shoes, Loki wheeled around and grabbed the goat's front hooves so it stood upright as he glared at it.

"Ha-ha! It looks like they're dancing together!" someone yelled. This idea was so silly that all the students cracked up. Always happy to be the center of attention, Loki began showing off, doing fancy steps with his hairy partner. That was the thing about Loki. No matter how badly he behaved, he could be so much fun at other times that everyone always forgave him.

Skade looked over to see Freya, Sif, and Idun waving at her to come dance with them. Confidence soaring, Skade bounced across the floor to join them and show off her moves. She even added in some modified ski jump stunts with leaps and twists. These moves were unconventional. One might even say they were *nontraditional*. But so what? Even if those moves never caught on with anyone else, it really didn't matter. Because she was having fun!

"Can you teach me how to do that?" begged a light-elf she didn't know well. "Me too," "Me three," some students chimed in.

Soon a whole crowd had gathered around her. Some clapped in time to Bragi's and Fossegrim's rollicking tunes while others tried their best to copy Skade's creative dances as she shifted from one novel move to another.

"I'm calling this one my Antler Dance," Skade told

everyone. So saying, she whipped out Ms. Frigg's antler beanie from her pocket and put it on. Seeing this, those from her ski team did the same. Students without these prized beanies made do by wiggling their fingers up by their ears as they leaped to and fro like deer.

Skade boogied with her podmates, by herself, and with anyone and everyone. She danced by Balder, then by Njord. Did she feel any extra-special excitement when she was around either of those boygods? Hmm. Right then, she decided she liked all of her friends more or less equally, though for different reasons. Like her boots, each had unique qualities. In the future, now and then, she might momentarily get that happy-melty feeling over a boy. But she wasn't going to worry about crushes. Someday, if one really, truly, finally happened to her, she was confident that her heart would know.

Skade smiled big. Thinking about what Odin and Ms. Frigg had said earlier, she was glad there would be another ski games in their future. Hooray! And in the months to come, she could look forward to more friendship and fun here at Asgard Academy.

As the night came to a close, she and her three podmates hugged one another before exiting the Valhallateria. On their way to the girls' dorm, she noticed that some students up ahead of them on the path were still practicing her Antler Dance moves. It made her glow with pleasure. It seemed she had started a *new* dance tradition!

Confidence is key, as Odin had told her. He'd been right!

"Let's dance home!" Skade suggested to Freya, Sif, and Idun.

"Yeah! Let's boogie!" her podmates shouted in reply.

Together they created a noisy, silly stomping dance. And they did it loud and proud all the way back to Vingolf. Because, why not? After all, they were the *Thunder* Girls!

Authors' Note

TO WRITE EACH BOOK IN THE THUNDER GIRLS series, we choose one or more Norse myths and then give them an updated middle-grade twist. After deciding on what elements we'll include from various retellings of the myths, we freely add interesting and funny details in order to create meaningful and entertaining stories we hope you'll enjoy.

We also write the Goddess Girls middle-grade series, which features Greek mythology. So why write another kind of mythology now too? Good question! Our enthusiasm for Norse mythology strengthened after Suzanne began frequent visits to her daughter and granddaughter, who live in Oslo, Norway. There, representations of the Norse gods and goddesses and their myths are found in many museums. Along the walls in the courtyard of the Oslo City Hall, there are painted wooden friezes (by painter and sculptor Dagfin Werenskiold) that illustrate motifs from various Norse myths. These friezes are the inspiration for the Valhallateria friezes that come alive at the end of meals in Thunder Girls!

We hope our series will motivate you to seek out actual retellings of Norse myths, which will also give you more understanding of and "inside information" about characters, myths, and details we've woven into Thunder Girls. Below are some of the sources we consult to create our stories.

- *D'Aulaires' Book of Norse Myths* by Ingri and Edgar Parin D'Aulaire (for young readers)
- *The Norse Myths* by Kevin Crossley-Holland
- *The Prose Edda* by Snorri Sturluson
- *The Poetic Edda* translated and edited by Jackson Crawford
- *Norse Mythology: A Guide to the Gods, Heroes, Rituals, and Beliefs* by John Lindow
- *Norse Mythology A to Z* by Kathleen N. Daly

For more about the art and friezes at Oslo City Hall, visit theoslobook.no/2016/09/03/oslo-city-hall.

Happy reading!

Joan and Suzanne

Acknowledgments

Many thanks to our publisher, Aladdin/Simon & Schuster, and our editor, Alyson Heller, who gave an immediate and supportive yes to our idea to write a Norse mythology–based middle-grade series. Alyson also edits Goddess Girls, Heroes in Training, and Little Goddess Girls, our three ongoing Greek mythology–based series for children. We have worked with her for many years and feel very lucky to be doing all these series with her and the other fine folk at Aladdin. They help make our words shine, design fabulous art to make our books stand out, and make every effort to see that our books reach as many readers as possible.

We are also indebted to our literary agent, Liza Voges. She has championed us in all our joint series ventures and worked hard on our behalf and on behalf of our books. Thank you, Liza!

We are grateful to artist Julio Cesar for his striking cover for this book in our Thunder Girls series.

Finally, we thank our husbands, George Hallowell and Mark Williams, for offering advice when asked, troubleshooting computer problems, and just making our lives richer and easier. During hectic times in our writing schedules they're always good sports, taking up the slack of daily chores without complaint.

Glossary

NOTE: **PARENTHESES INCLUDE INFORMATION** specific to the Thunder Girls series.

Aesir: Norse goddesses and gods who live in Asgard

Alfheim: World on the first (top) ring where light-elves live

Angerboda: Loki's giantess wife whose name means "distress-bringer" (angry Asgard Academy student and girlgiant)

Asgard: World on the first (top) ring where Aesir goddesses and gods live

Balder: Beloved Aesir god of peace and light whose skin glows (popular Asgard Academy student and boygod)

Bifrost Bridge: Red, blue, and green rainbow bridge built by the Aesir from fire, air, and water

Breidablik Hall: Hall of the Norse god Balder (boys' dorm at Asgard Academy)

Brising: Freya's necklace, shortened from *Brísingamen* (Freya's magic jewel)

Darkalfheim: World on the second (middle) ring where dwarfs live

Dwarfs: Short blacksmiths in Darkalfheim (some young dwarfs attend Asgard Academy)

Fire giants: Terrifying giants that live in Muspelheim

Frey: Vanir god of agriculture and fertility whose name is sometimes spelled Freyr, brother of Freya (Freya's twin brother and Asgard Academy student and boygod)

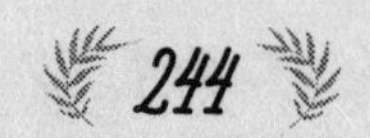

Freya: Vanir goddess of love and fertility (Vanir girlgoddess of love and beauty who is an Asgard Academy student)

Frigg: Goddess of marriage, who is Odin's wife (coprincipal of Asgard Academy with Odin)

Frost giants: Descendants of Ymir from Jotunheim

Gladsheim Hall: Sanctuary where twelve Norse gods hold meetings (Asgard Academy's assembly hall)

Gullveig: Vanir sorceress (Freya and Frey's nanny and library assistant at the Heartwood Library)

***Hangerock*:** Sleeveless apronlike dress, with shoulder straps that are fastened in front by clasps, that is worn over a long-sleeved linen shift

Heimdall: Watchman of the gods (security guard at Asgard Academy)

Helheim: World on the third (bottom) ring inhabited by the some of the dead and ruled by a female monster named Hel

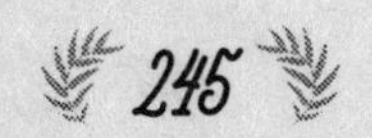

Hugin: One of Odin's two ravens whose name means "thought"

Idun: Aesir goddess who is the keeper of the golden apples of youth (Asgard Academy student and girl-goddess)

***Jotun*:** Norse word for "giant"

Jotunheim: World on the second (middle) ring where frost giants live

Light-elves: Happy Asgard Academy students from Alfheim

Loki: Troublemaking, shape-shifting god of fire (Asgard Academy student and boygod)

Midgard: World on the second (middle) ring where humans live

Mimir: Wise Aesir god who was beheaded and revived by Odin ("head" librarian at Asgard Academy)

Mjollnir: Mighty hammer made for Thor

Munin: One of Odin's two ravens whose name means "memory"

Muspelheim: World on the third (bottom) ring where fire giants live

Nidhogg: Dragon that lives in Niflheim and gnaws at the root of the World Tree

Niflheim: World on the third (bottom) ring where the good dead are sent

Njord: Vanir god of the sea sent to Asgard after the Aesir-Vanir war (Asgard Academy student and boy-god from Vanaheim)

Norse: Related to the ancient people of Scandinavia, a region in Northern Europe that includes Denmark, Norway, and Sweden and sometimes Finland, Iceland, and the Faroe Islands

Odin: Powerful Norse god of war, wisdom, and poetry who watches over all nine worlds (coprincipal of Asgard Academy with his wife, Ms. Frigg)

Ragnarok: Prophesied doomsday when goddesses and gods will fight a fiery battle against evil that could destroy all nine Norse worlds

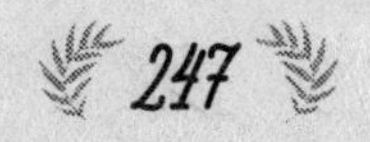

Ratatosk: Squirrel that runs up and down Yggdrasil spreading gossip and insults

Sif: Golden-haired goddess of the harvest (Asgard Academy student and girlgoddess)

Skade: Goddess of skiing, sometimes spelled Skadi (Asgard Academy student and half-giant girl)

***Skidbladnir*:** Magical ship made as a gift for Frey

Skrymir: A frost giant in Jotunheim who can create magical illusions and likes to annoy the Norse gods

Snorri Sturluson: Author of a famous book about Norse History called the *Prose Edda* (Norse History teacher at Asgard Academy)

Surt: A warrior fire giant from Muspelheim who wields a fiery sword and will one day lead the battle of Ragnarok against the Norse gods

Thor: Superstrong Norse god of thunder and storms (Asgard Academy student and boygod)

Ull: Norse god associated with archery and snow skiing (Asgard Academy student and boygod)

Valhalla: Huge room in Asgard where dead warriors feast and fight (Valhallateria is Asgard Academy's cafeteria)

Valkyries: Warrior maidens in winged helmets who choose which warriors will die in battle and then bring them to Valhalla (cafeteria ladies and workers in Asgard Academy's Valhallateria)

Vanaheim: World on the first (top) ring where Vanir goddesses and gods live

Vanir: Norse goddesses and gods who live in Vanaheim

Vingolf Hall: Goddesses' meeting hall at Asgard (girls' dorm at Asgard Academy)

Yggdrasil: Enormous ash tree that links all nine ancient Norse worlds, also called the World Tree (location of Asgard Academy)

Ymir: Very first frost giant whose body parts were used to create the Norse cosmos, including mountains, the sea, and the heavens

Don't miss the first
Thunder Girls adventure!

Jewel

MEOW! MEOW!

"Fly, kitty, kitty!" the girlgoddess Freya called to her magical gray tabby cats. Her long pale-blond hair fanned out behind her as she urged them onward. The red cart they pulled soared a half-dozen feet above the snowy ground, around tree trunks and under branches, sometimes barely missing big, mossy boulders. It wasn't easy to get this pair of pony-size cats to fly the cart in the direction she wanted them to go!

Upon reaching a familiar forest path lined with ferns, she called out, “Whoa, kitty, kitty!” To her relief, the cats obeyed and set down in the snow. “Good job, *silfrkatter*,” she said, using the Norse word that meant “silver cats.” “Our first trip together. And we made it!” She leaned forward to pat the cats’ soft fur, and they purred happily.

Remembering why she’d come all this way, Freya jumped from the cart and commanded, “Catnap!”

Plink! If anyone had been watching at that moment, the cats and cart would’ve seemed to instantly disappear. However, in reality, they had only shrunk down to a single cat’s-eye marble. Freya’s twin brother, the boygod Frey, had given her the colorful marble as a gift only yesterday, on her twelfth birthday.

She snatched the marble from the air before it could fall to the snowy ground. Then she slipped it into one of several fist-size pouches that dangled from the nine necklaces of beads, seeds, or metal chain that she wore. Each necklace held one or more items, such as keys, small tools, or special keepsakes.

Nine was a lucky, super-special number. Because as everyone knew, there were nine worlds altogether in the Norse universe. All were located on three enormous, ring-shaped levels stacked one above the other. Vanaheim, the world where Freya lived, was only *one* of those worlds!

Freya's breath made quick fog-puffs in the cold air as she crossed the path and stepped into a small hut. It was the home of the old sorceress Gullveig, who she and her brother called *amma*. That meant "grandmother," though Gullveig was really their nanny, not a relative. Once inside, Freya saw that the hut was still as empty as it had been for the last five months. Her shoulders slumped in disappointment.

She pulled a walnut-size jewel shaped like a teardrop from another necklace pouch and stared at it. It was pale orange now, which meant it felt unsettled, like she did. While in her possession, it changed colors according to her mood!

"Tell me, jewel Brising, where is Gullveig?" she asked it. "Did she find the gold she was looking for in Asgard?"

Her jewel's voice came as a low, magical humming sound that only she could hear and understand:

"Gold and Gullveig I cannot see.
But here is the vision that comes to me:
Adventure for you is about to start.
In Asgard you must find the heart.
A secret world there hides away
That holds the power to stop doomsday!"

Startled, Freya stared at the teardrop jewel. "Secret world? Doomsday? I'm not going to Asgard. I'm not! What are you talking about, Brising?" She brought the jewel so close to her nose that her blue eyes almost crossed, wanting it to take back what it had said. It didn't. Although it had the power to show Freya the future, sometimes it only revealed bits of information. It didn't always answer her questions, either, so she could never be sure what it did or didn't know. This time, though, she was positive it was wrong, wrong, wrong. Why would she ever leave Vanaheim? She loved it here!

As Freya stepped out of the hut into the cold air, Brising spoke up again, though she had asked it nothing more. This time it said:

> *"Five months ago a war began.*
> *Five days ago that fight did end.*
> *Five hours ago your fate was sealed—*
> *Five minutes from now 'twill be revealed.*
> *Oops, make that five seconds from now.*
> *One. Two. Three. Four. . . ."*